KING ARTHUR
AND THE KNIGHTS OF THE
ROUND TABLE

A GRAPHIC NOVEL

BY M.C. HALL &
C.E. RICHARDS

STONE ARCH BOOKS
A CAPSTONE IMPRINT

Graphic Revolve is published by Stone Arch Books
A Capstone Imprint
1710 Roe Crest Drive, North Mankato, Minnesota 56003
www.capstonepub.com

First published in 2006.

Cataloging-in-Publication Data is available at the Library
of Congress website.
Hardcover ISBN: 978-1-4965-0006-9
Paperback ISBN: 978-1-4965-0025-0

Summary: In a world of wizards, giants, and dragons,
King Arthur and the Knights of the Round Table are the
only defense against the forces of evil that threaten the
kingdom of Camelot.

Common Core back matter written by Dr. Katie Monnin.

Designer: Bob Lentz
Assistant Designer: Peggie Carley
Editor: Donald Lemke
Assistant Editor: Sean Tulien
Creative Director: Heather Kindseth
Editorial Director: Michael Dahl
Publisher: Ashley C. Andersen Zantop

Printed and bound in China.   PO4399

TABLE OF CONTENTS

ABOUT KING ARTHUR

The story of King Arthur is an ancient legend that storytellers passed down for many generations. The story was first told sometime before the 11th century. Finally, in the 15th century, Sir Thomas Malory wrote down his version of these stories. He titled the collection *The Book of King Arthur and His Noble Knights of the Round Table*.

People know little about Malory's interest in the stories of King Arthur. He likely heard different versions of these stories when he was growing up. Perhaps his life experience as a knight helped him better understand the King Arthur stories.

The stories of *King Arthur and the Knights of the Round Table* take place in Britain during the Middle Ages, a time period that lasted from the 5th to the 15th century CE. This was a period of unrest in Britain and Europe as people fought many wars for control of the land. Britain wasn't a united country at the time. Kings and lords throughout what is now England, Wales, and Scotland ruled over small regions scattered across the countryside.

Many people wonder if the legends of King Arthur are real and if the places in the story really existed. Some historians believe that the castle Camelot and the island of Avalon are based on real places in England. For example, some people believe that Arthur is buried beneath the town of Glastonbury. Visitors still travel to England to retrace the supposed steps of King Arthur and his knights.

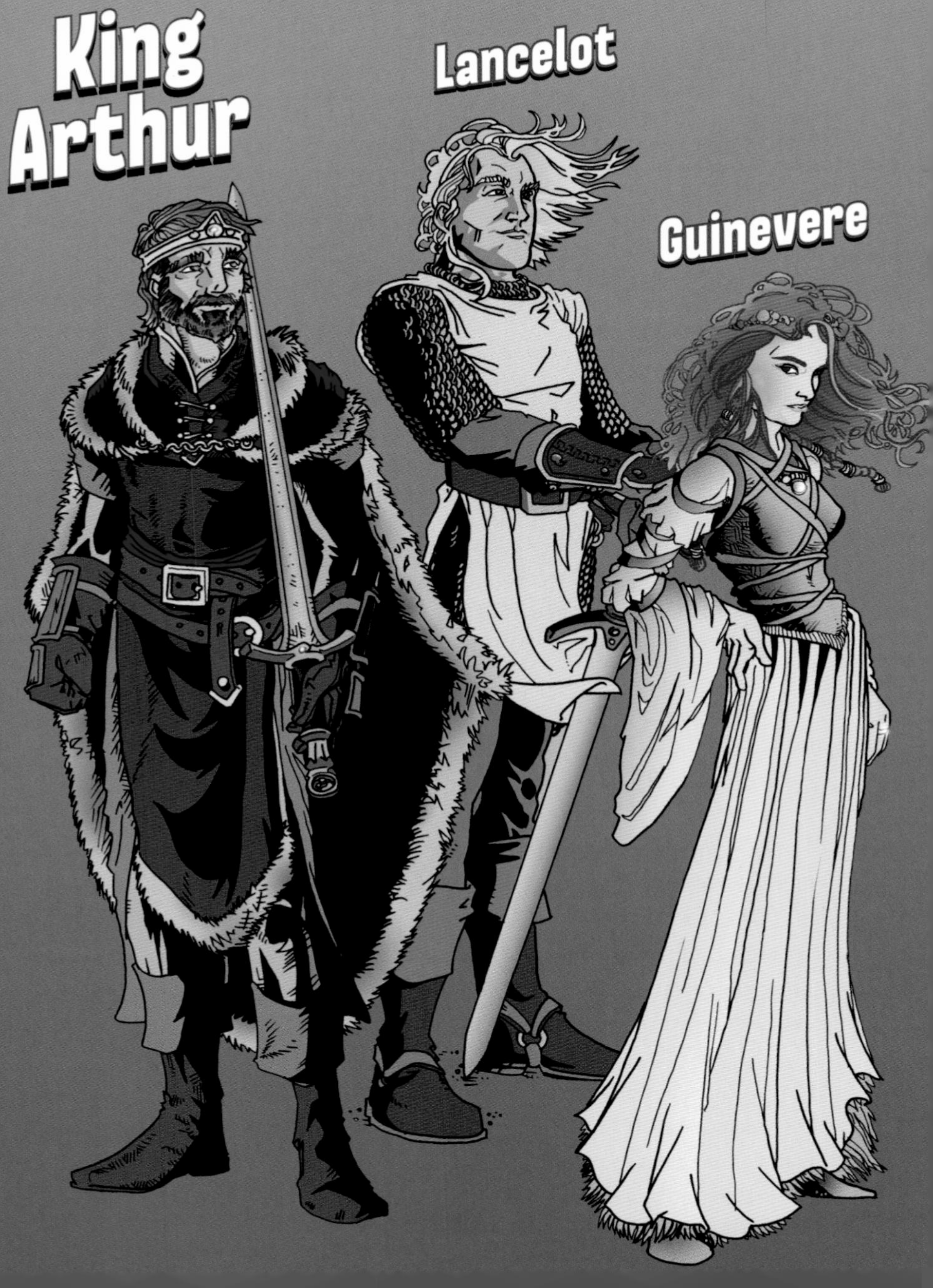
King Arthur
Lancelot
Guinevere

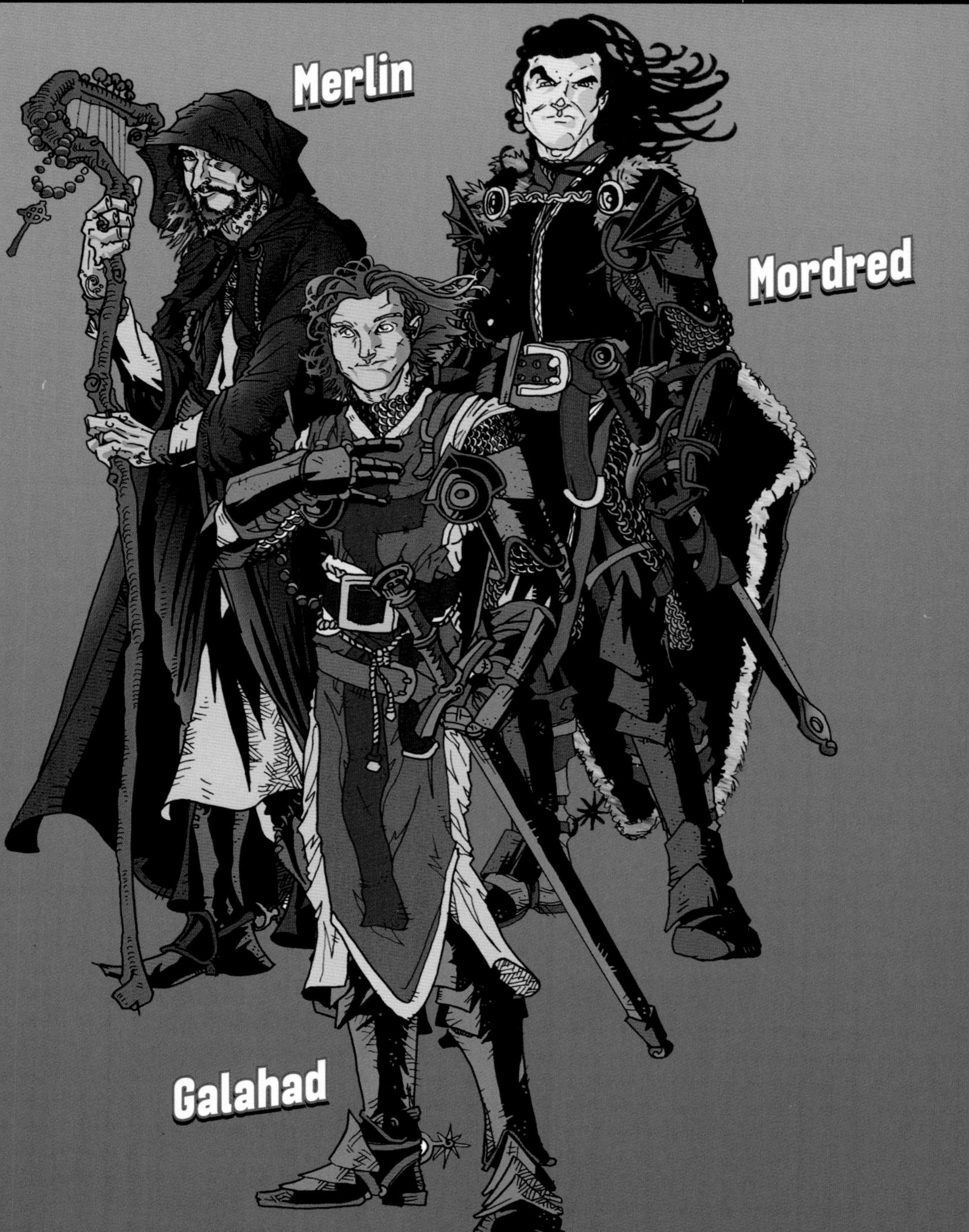
Merlin
Mordred
Galahad

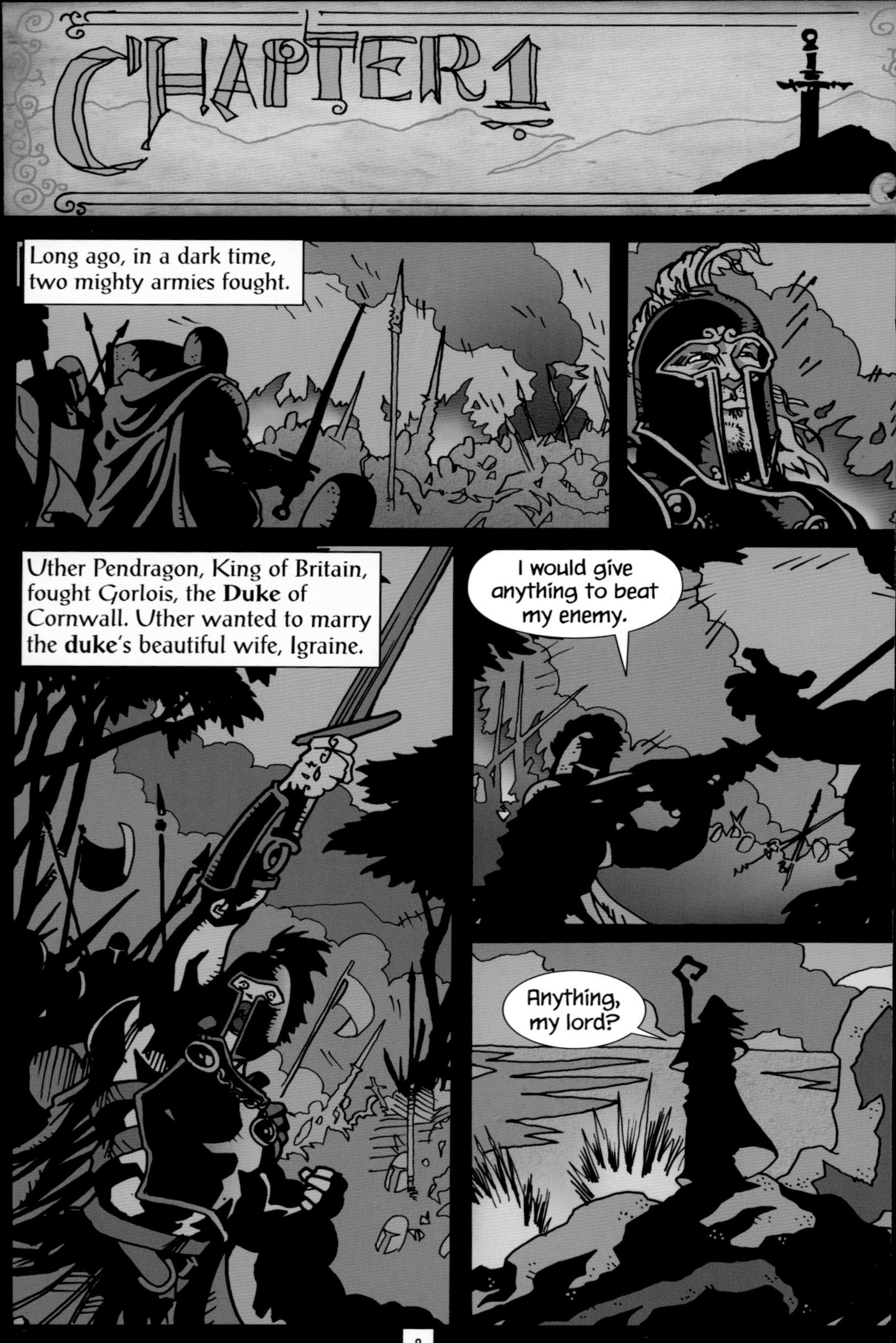
CHAPTER 1
Long ago, in a dark time, two mighty armies fought.
Uther Pendragon, King of Britain, fought Gorlois, the **Duke** of Cornwall. Uther wanted to marry the **duke**'s beautiful wife, Igraine.
I would give anything to beat my enemy.
Anything, my lord?

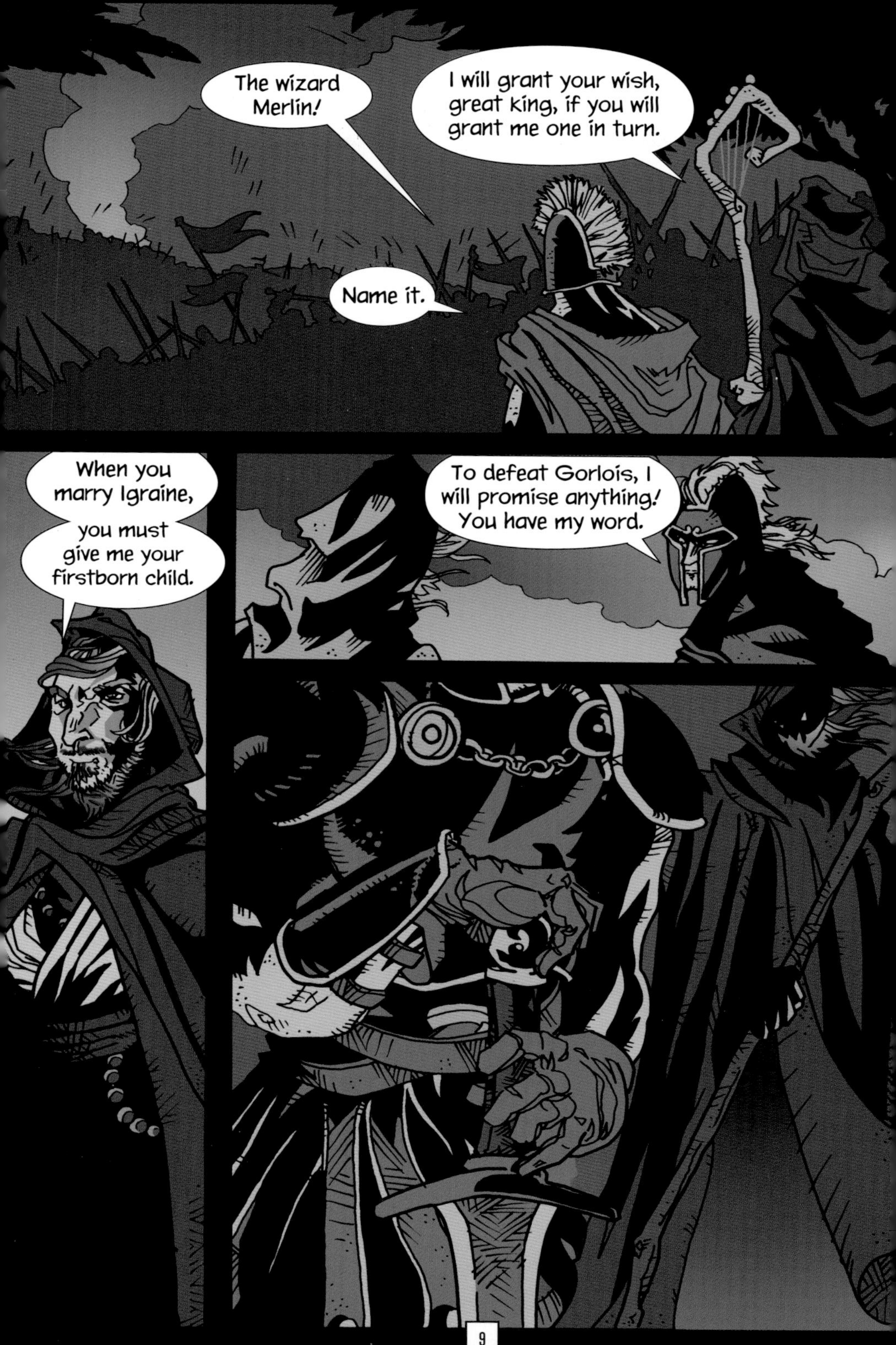
The wizard Merlin!
I will grant your wish, great king, if you will grant me one in turn.
Name it.
When you marry Igraine,
you must give me your firstborn child.
To defeat Gorlois, I will promise anything! You have my word.

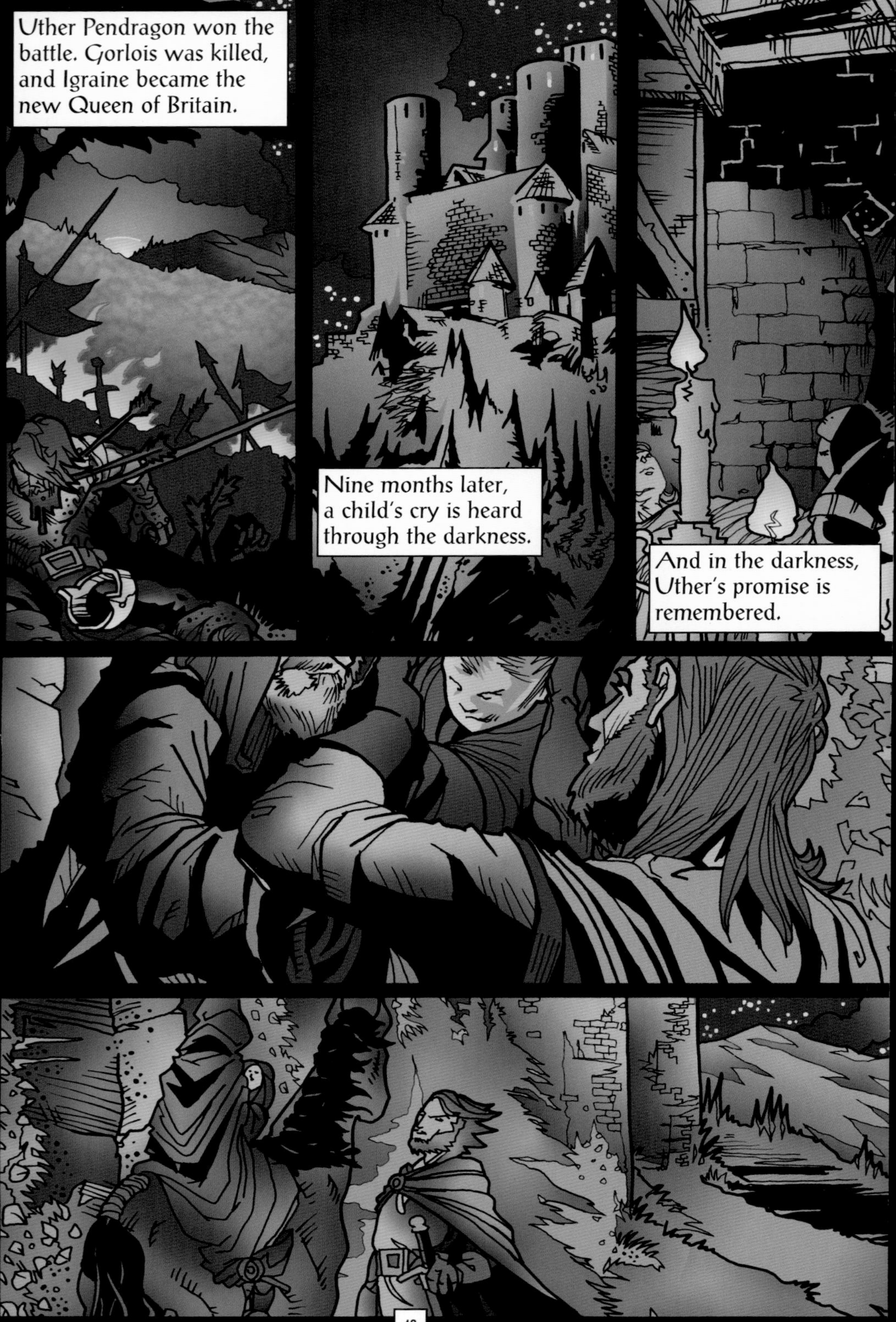
Uther Pendragon won the battle. Gorlois was killed, and Igraine became the new Queen of Britain.
Nine months later, a child's cry is heard through the darkness.
And in the darkness, Uther's promise is remembered.

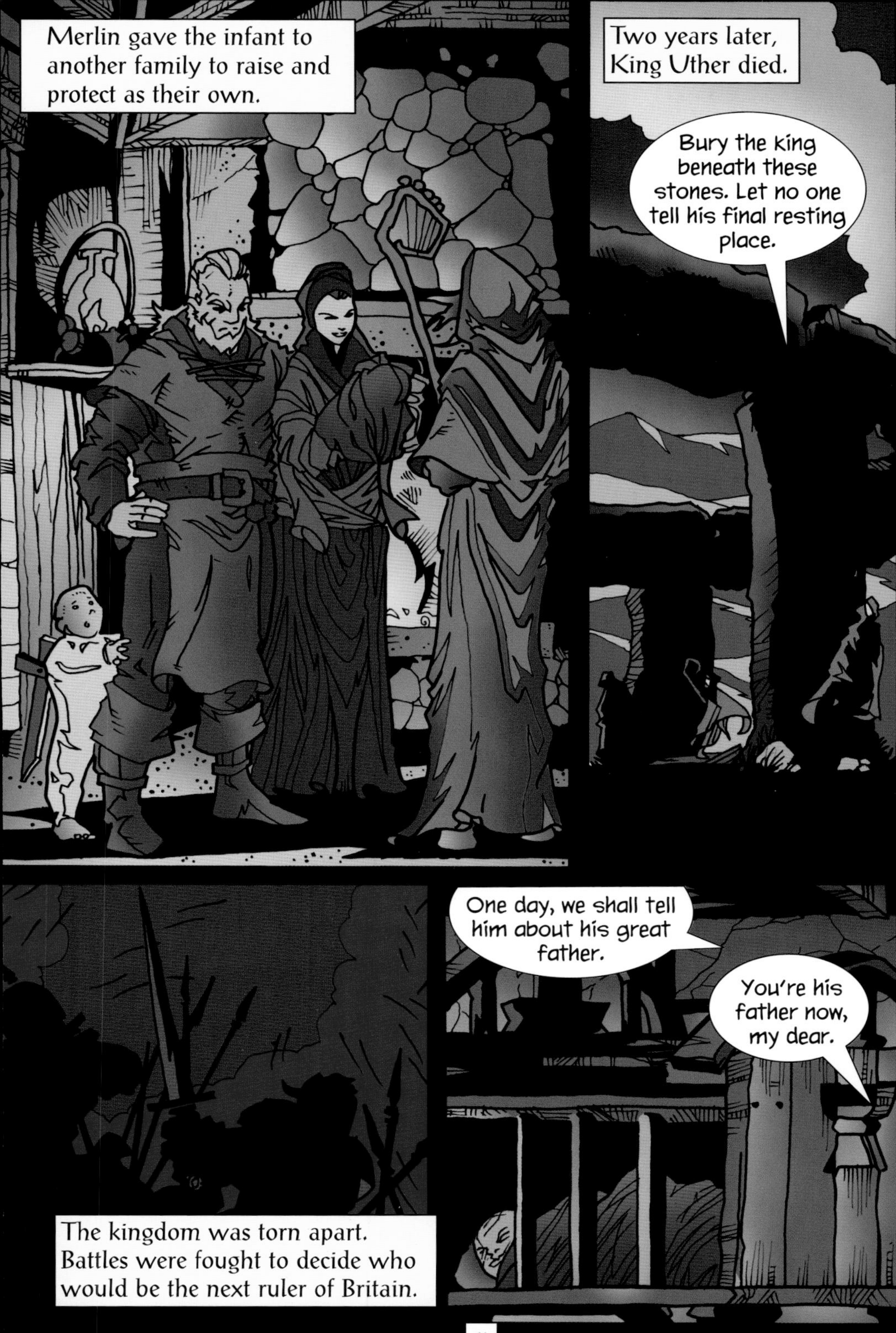
Merlin gave the infant to another family to raise and protect as their own.
Two years later, King Uther died.
Bury the king beneath these stones. Let no one tell his final resting place.
The kingdom was torn apart. Battles were fought to decide who would be the next ruler of Britain.
One day, we shall tell him about his great father.
You're his father now, my dear.

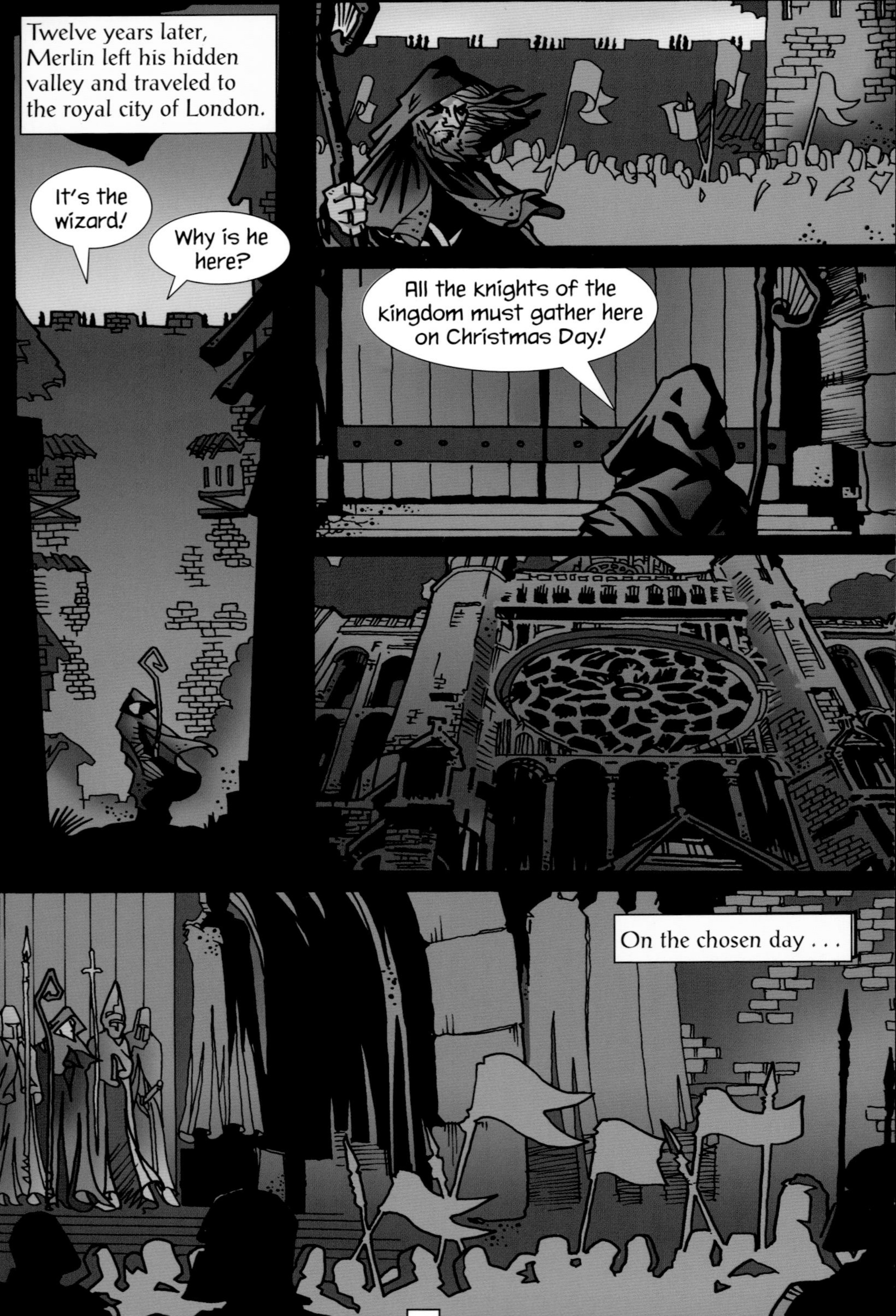
Twelve years later, Merlin left his hidden valley and traveled to the royal city of London.
It's the wizard!
Why is he here?
All the knights of the kingdom must gather here on Christmas Day!
On the chosen day . . .

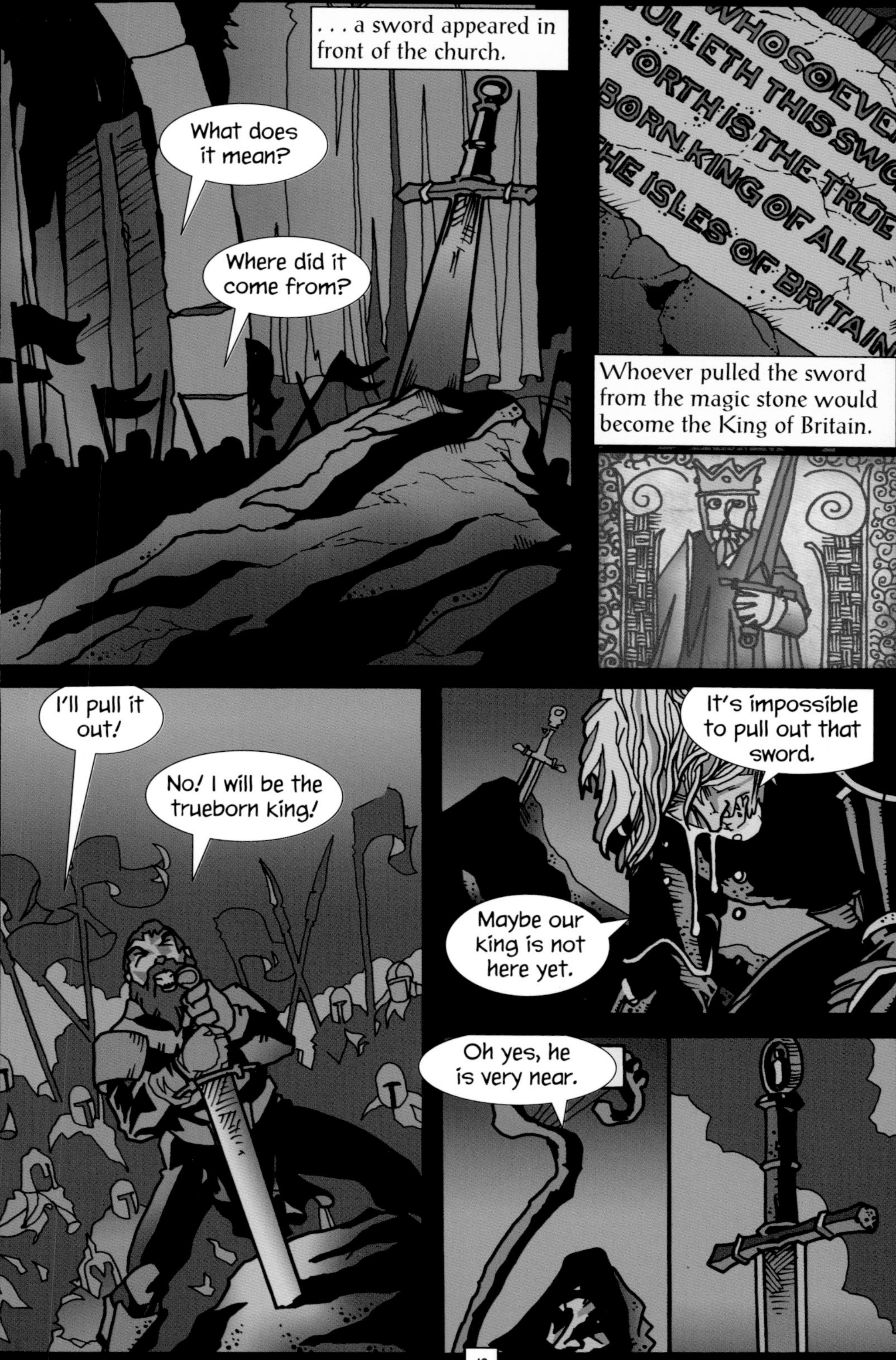

. . . a sword appeared in front of the church.
What does it mean?
Where did it come from?
WHOSOEVE
ULLETH THIS SWO
FORTH IS THE TRUE
BORN KING OF ALL
HE ISLES OF BRITAIN
Whoever pulled the sword from the magic stone would become the King of Britain.
I'll pull it out!
No! I will be the trueborn king!
It's impossible to pull out that sword.
Maybe our king is not here yet.
Oh yes, he is very near.

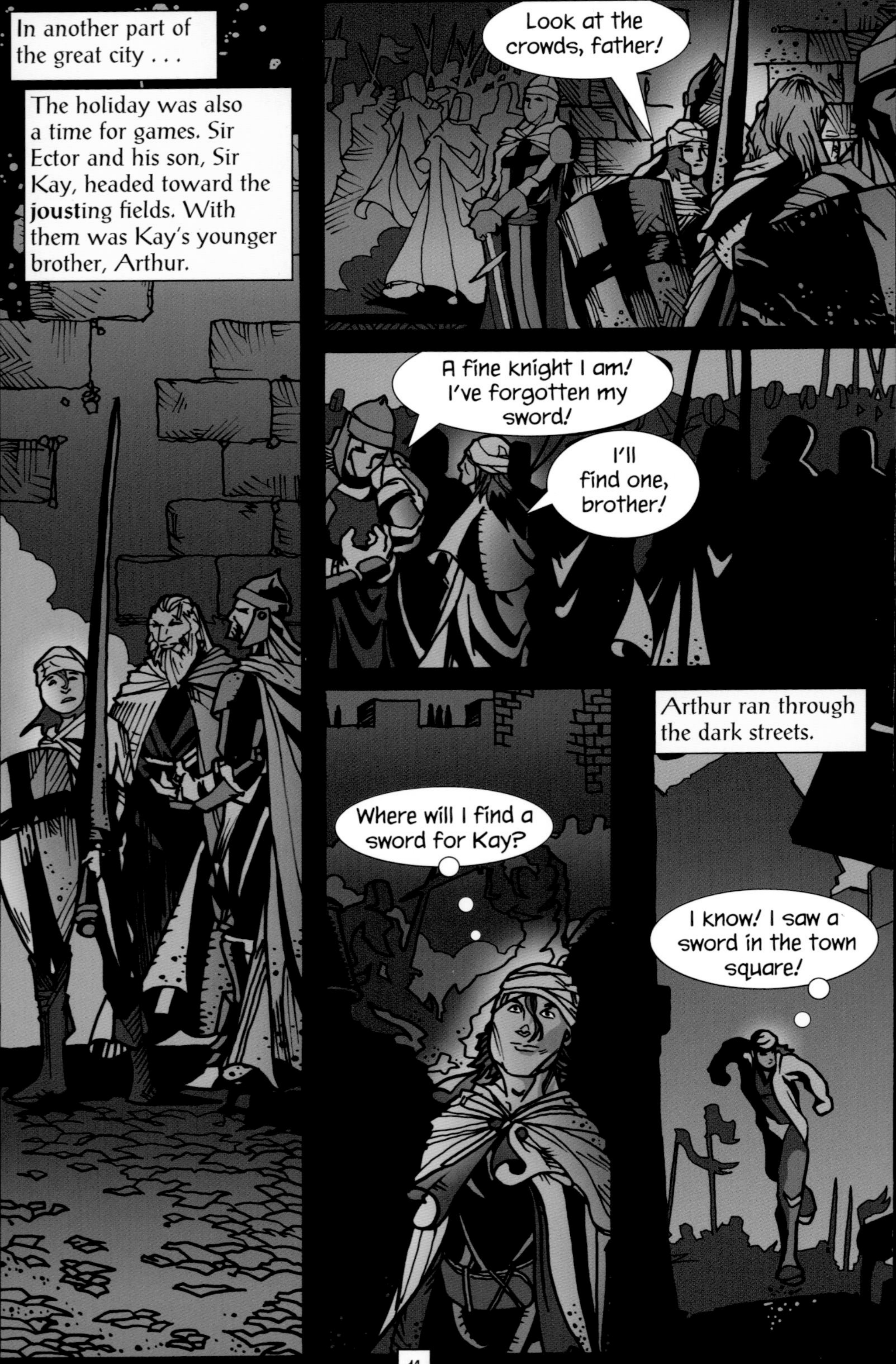
In another part of the great city . . .
The holiday was also a time for games. Sir Ector and his son, Sir Kay, headed toward the **jous**ting fields. With them was Kay's younger brother, Arthur.
Look at the crowds, father!
A fine knight I am! I've forgotten my sword!
I'll find one, brother!
Where will I find a sword for Kay?
Arthur ran through the dark streets.
I know! I saw a sword in the town square!

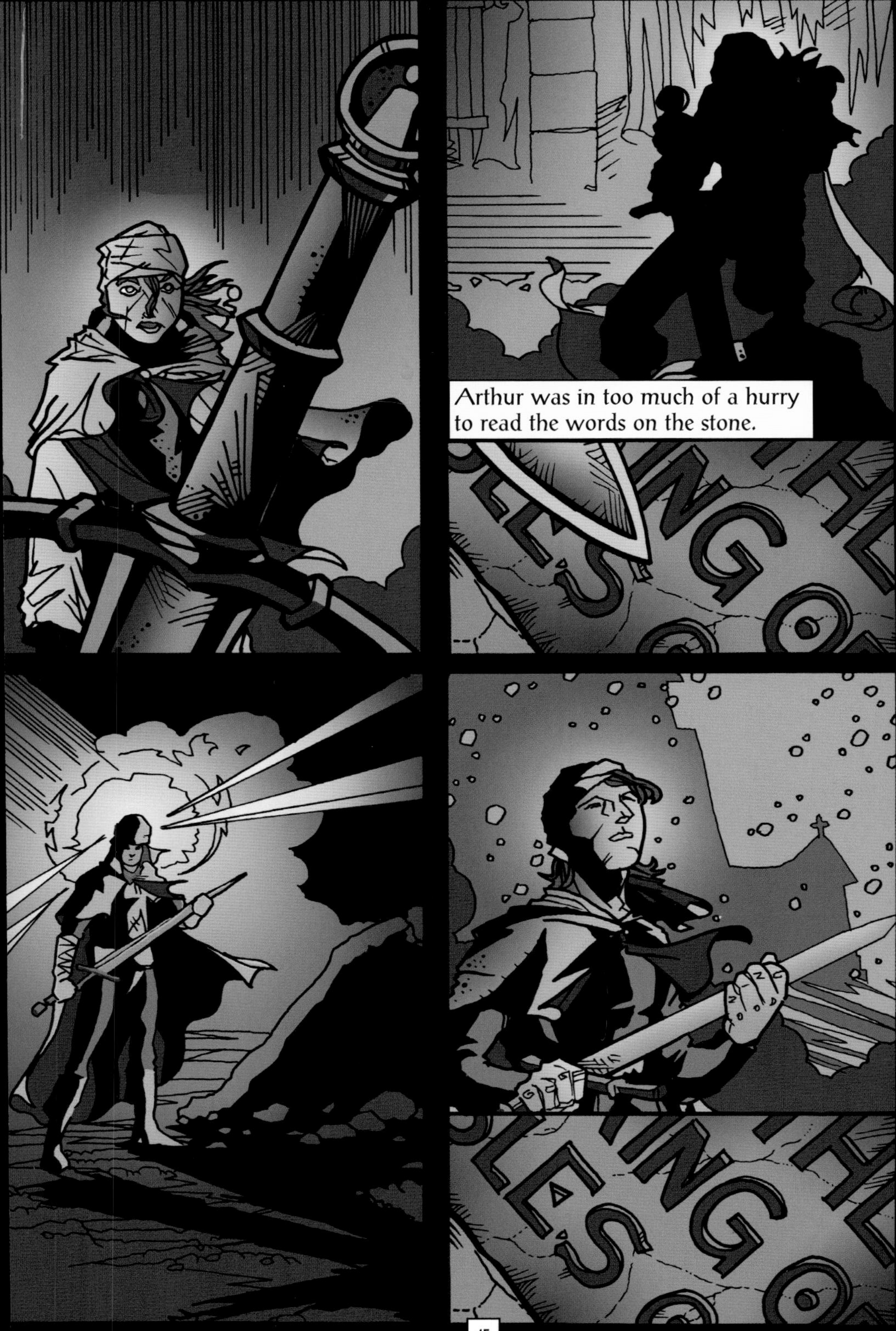
Arthur was in too much of a hurry to read the words on the stone.

Arthur hurried back to his father and brother.

It's the sword from the stone!

Sir Kay knew the sword at once. He had already tried to pull it from the stone.

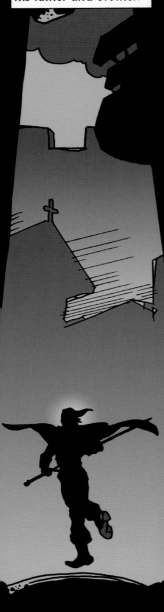

How did you get this, Arthur? We must return to the town square!

Kay needed a sword, Father. I remembered seeing this one. I was only going to borrow it.

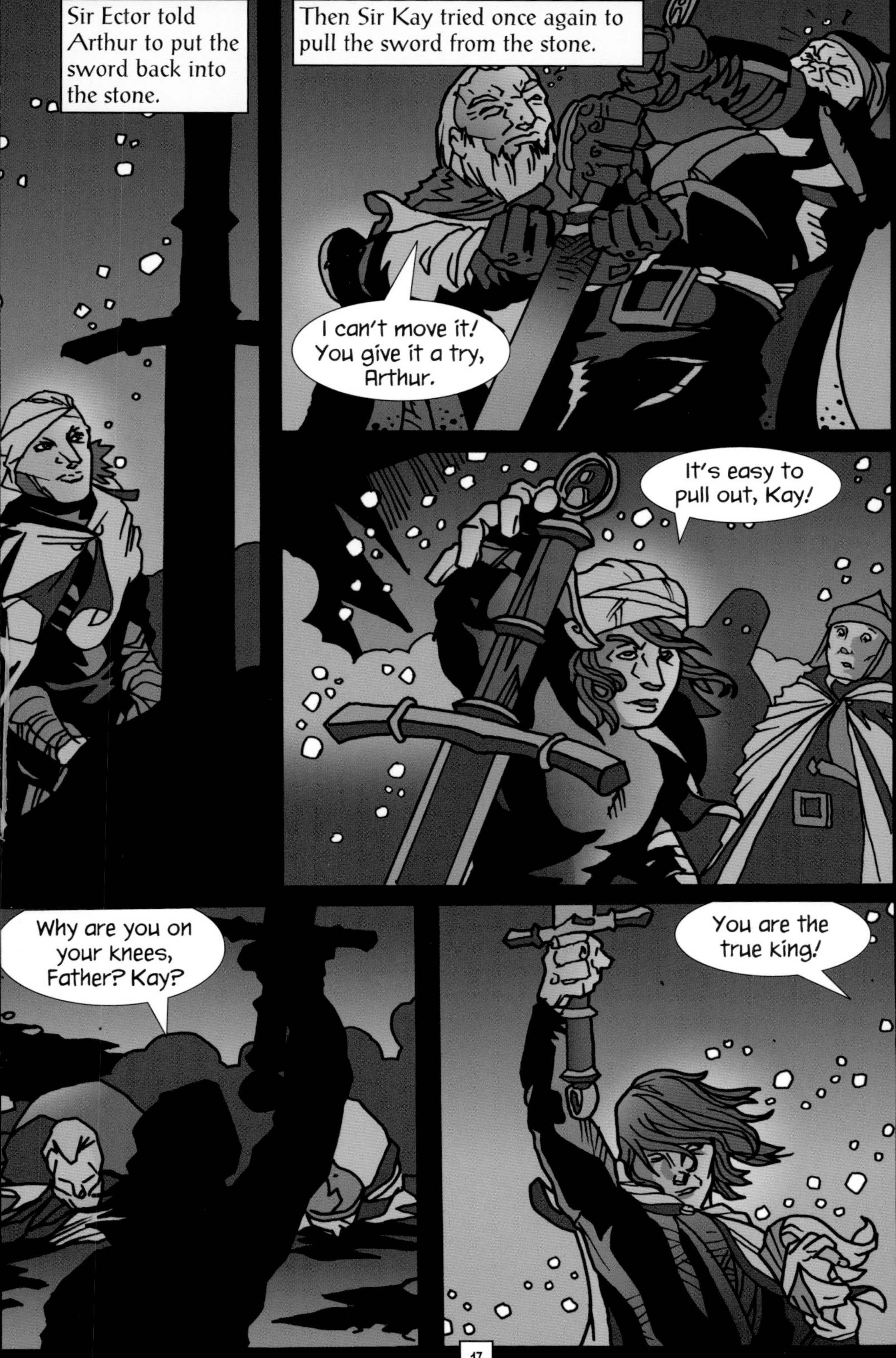
Sir Ector told Arthur to put the sword back into the stone.
Then Sir Kay tried once again to pull the sword from the stone.
I can't move it! You give it a try, Arthur.
It's easy to pull out, Kay!
Why are you on your knees, Father? Kay?
You are the true king!

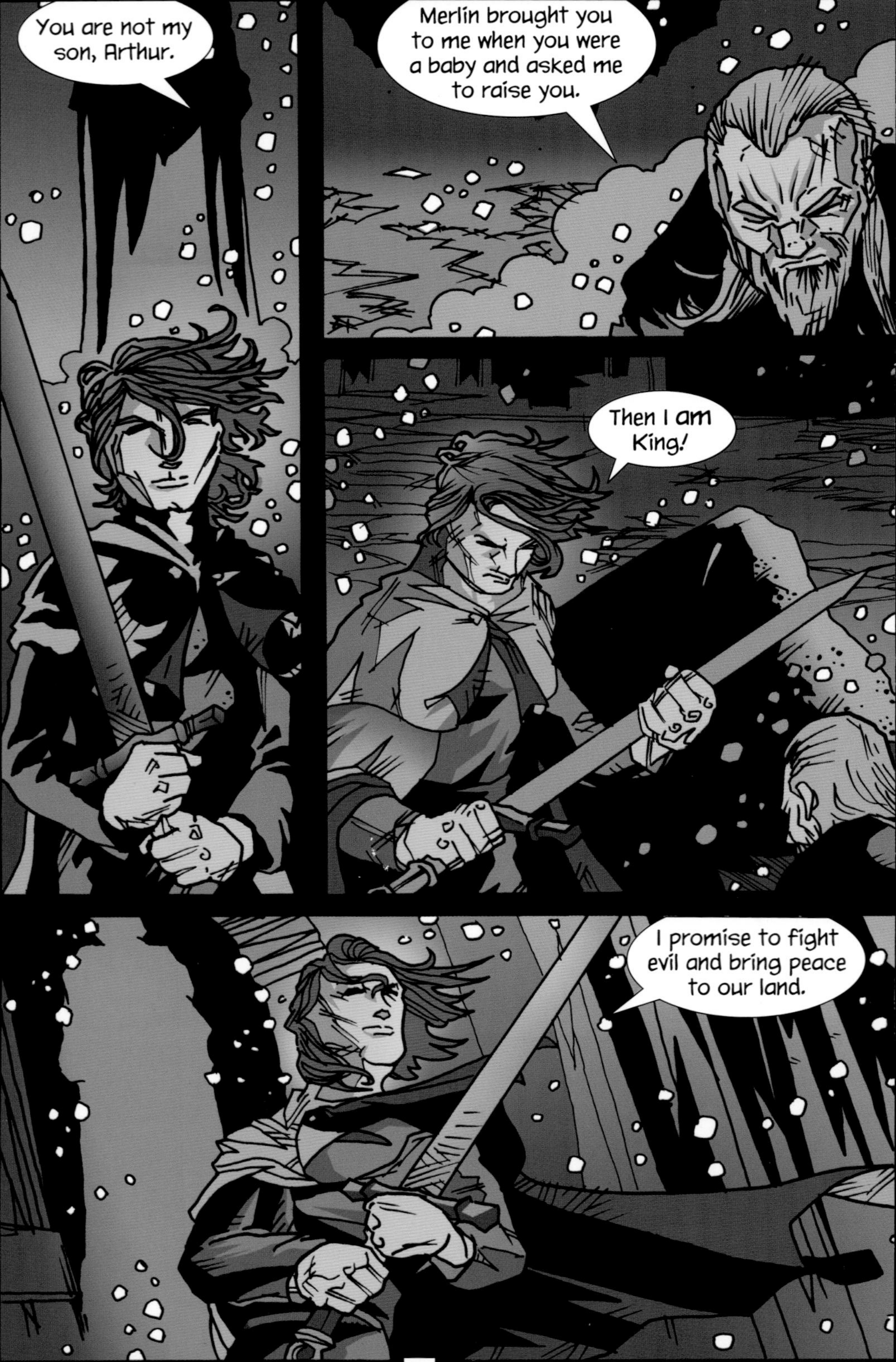

You are not my son, Arthur.
Merlin brought you to me when you were a baby and asked me to raise you.
Then I am King!
I promise to fight evil and bring peace to our land.

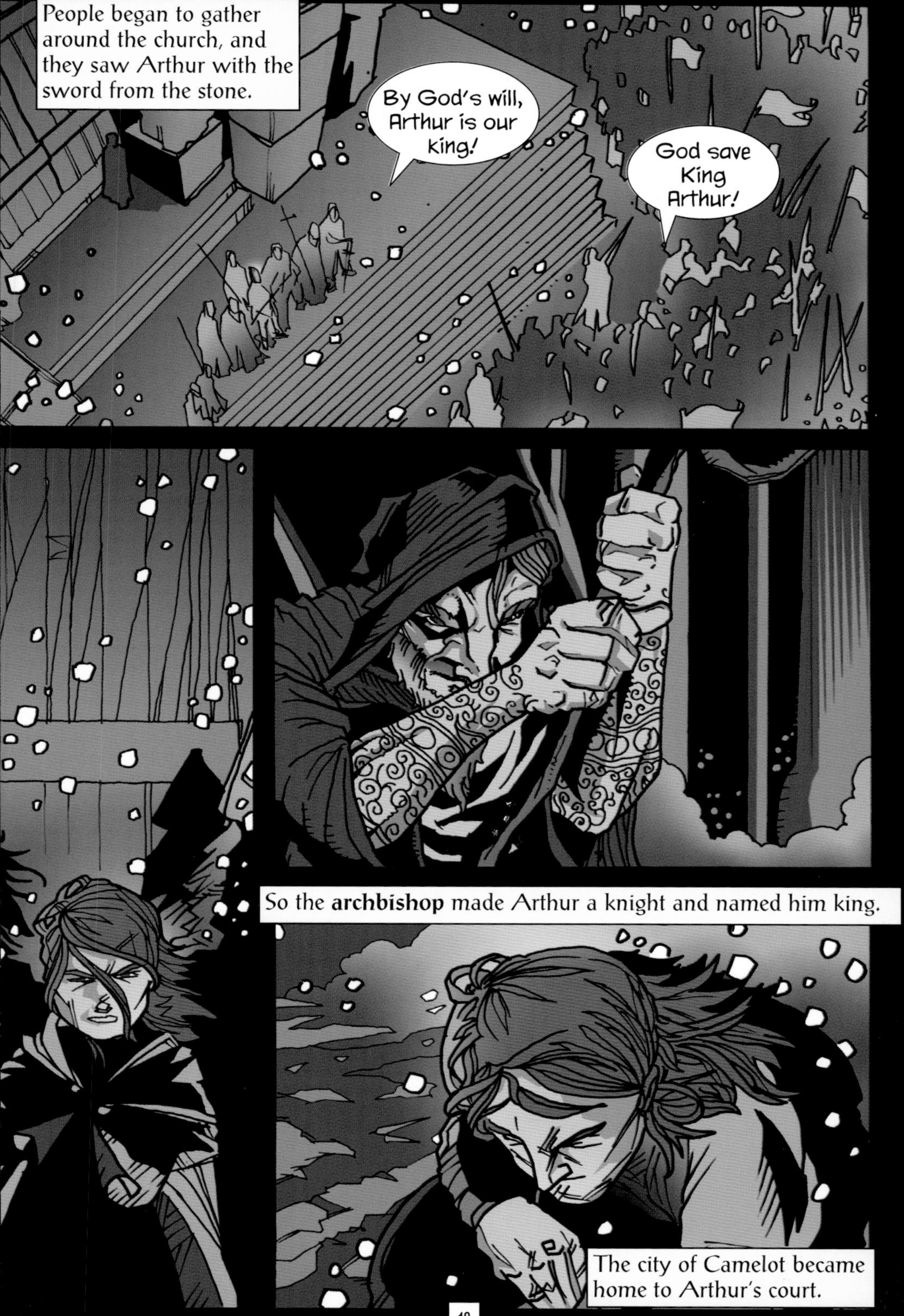
People began to gather around the church, and they saw Arthur with the sword from the stone.
By God's will, Arthur is our king!
God save King Arthur!
So the **archbishop** made Arthur a knight and named him king.
The city of Camelot became home to Arthur's court.

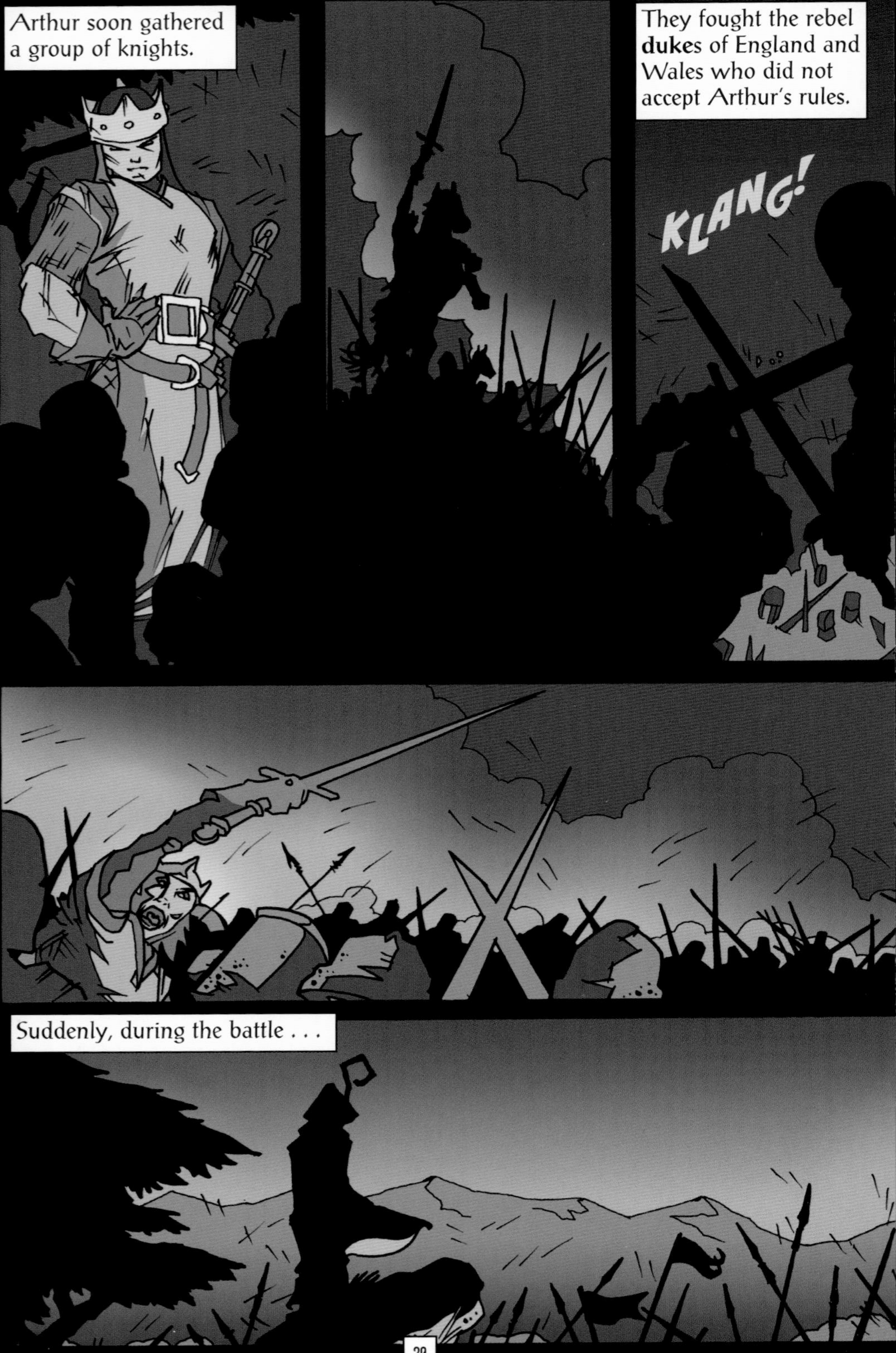
Arthur soon gathered a group of knights.
They fought the rebel **duke**s of England and Wales who did not accept Arthur's rules.
KLANG!
Suddenly, during the battle . . .

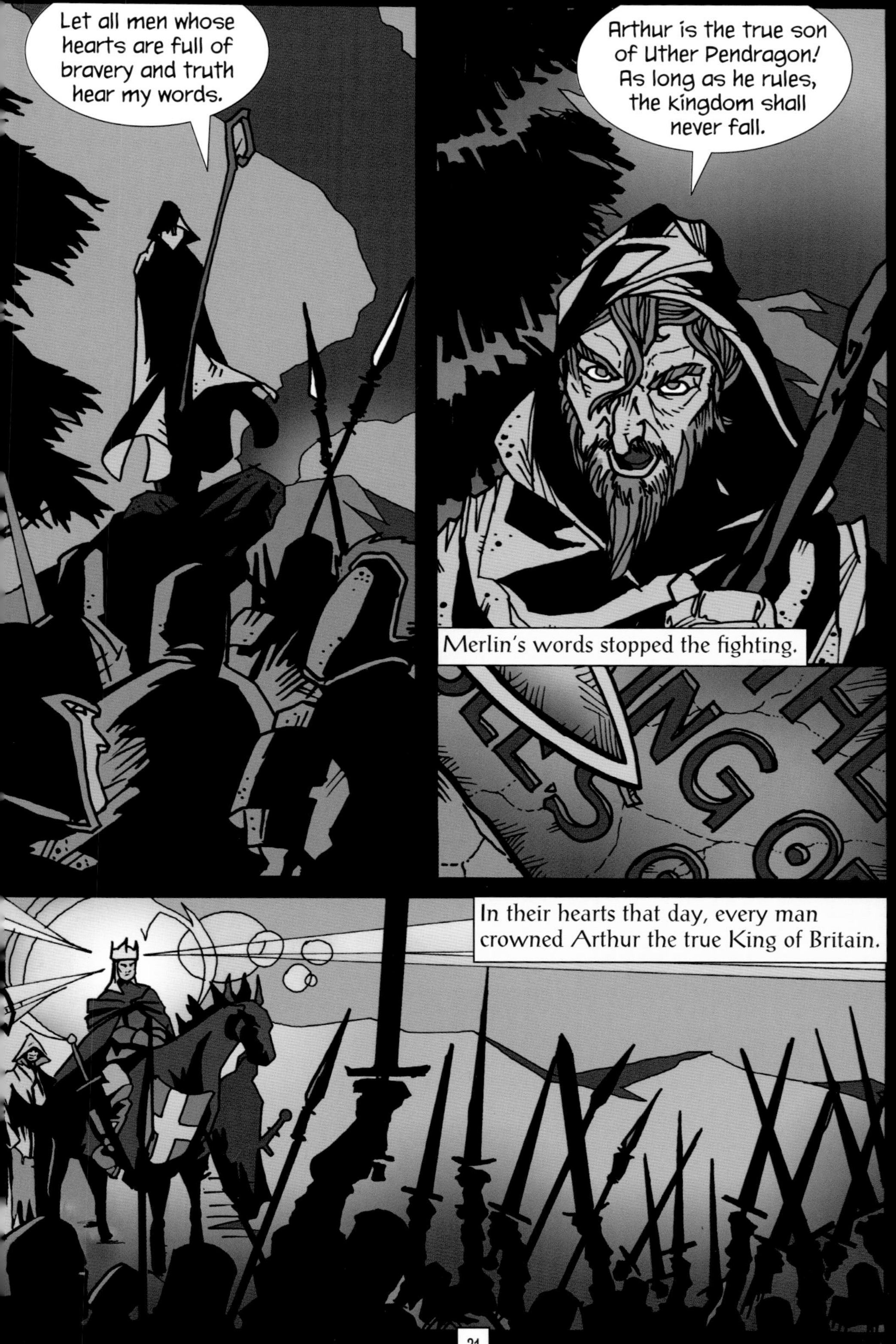
Let all men whose hearts are full of bravery and truth hear my words.
Arthur is the true son of Uther Pendragon! As long as he rules, the kingdom shall never fall.
Merlin's words stopped the fighting.
In their hearts that day, every man crowned Arthur the true King of Britain.

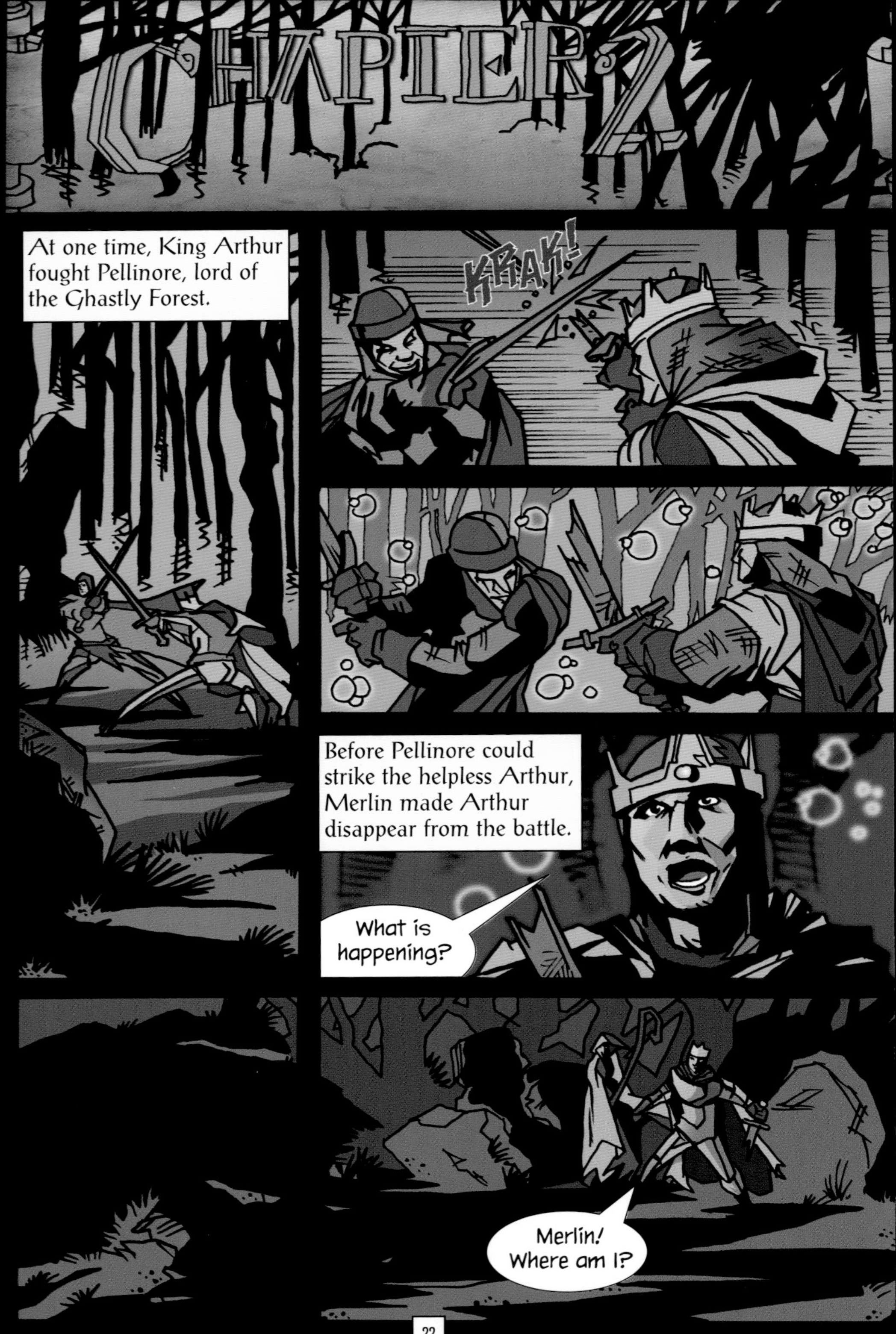
CHAPTER 2
At one time, King Arthur fought Pellinore, lord of the Ghastly Forest.
KRAK!
Before Pellinore could strike the helpless Arthur, Merlin made Arthur disappear from the battle.
What is happening?
Merlin! Where am I?

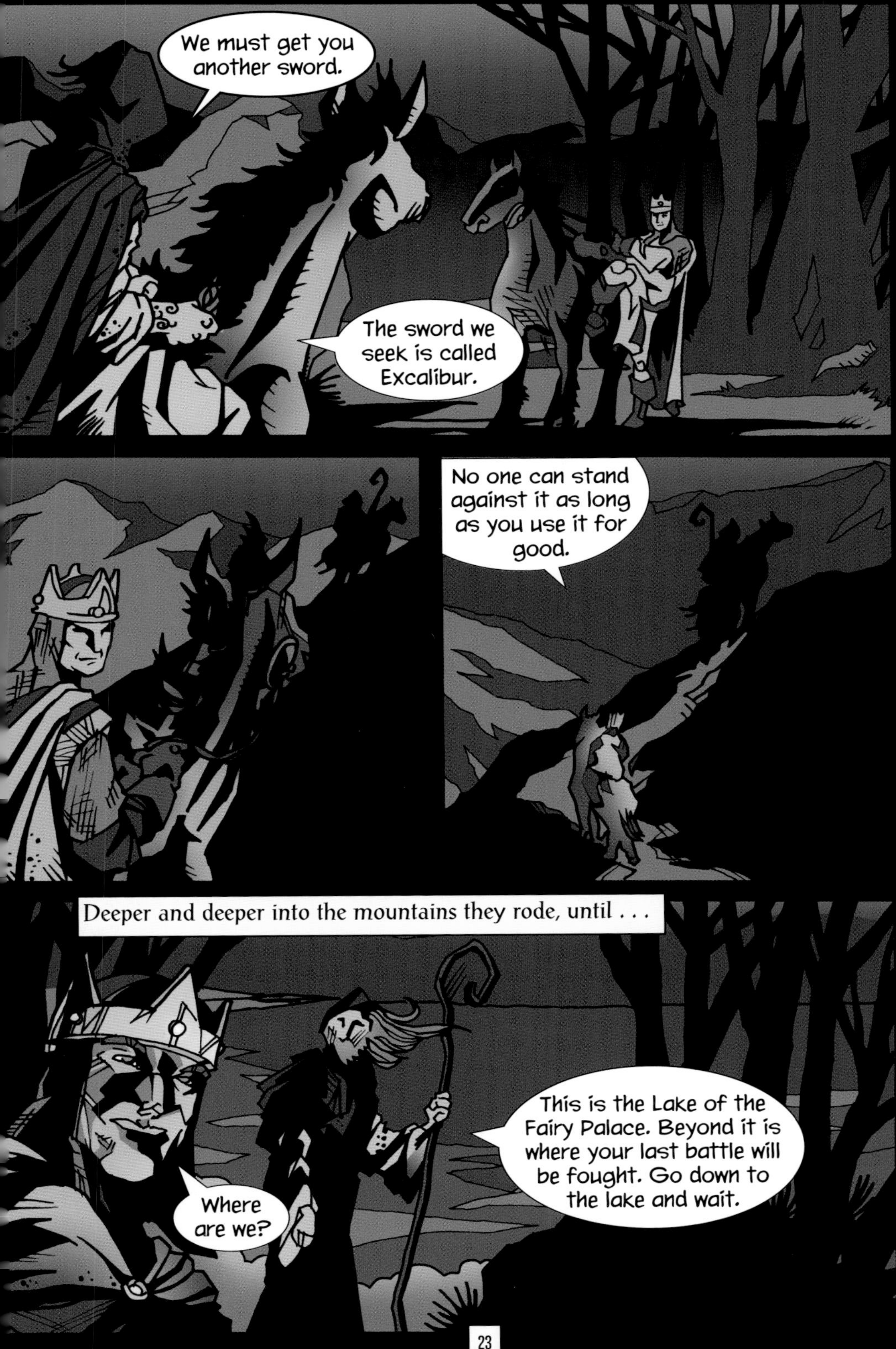

We must get you another sword.
The sword we seek is called Excalibur.
No one can stand against it as long as you use it for good.
Deeper and deeper into the mountains they rode, until . . .
Where are we?
This is the Lake of the Fairy Palace. Beyond it is where your last battle will be fought. Go down to the lake and wait.

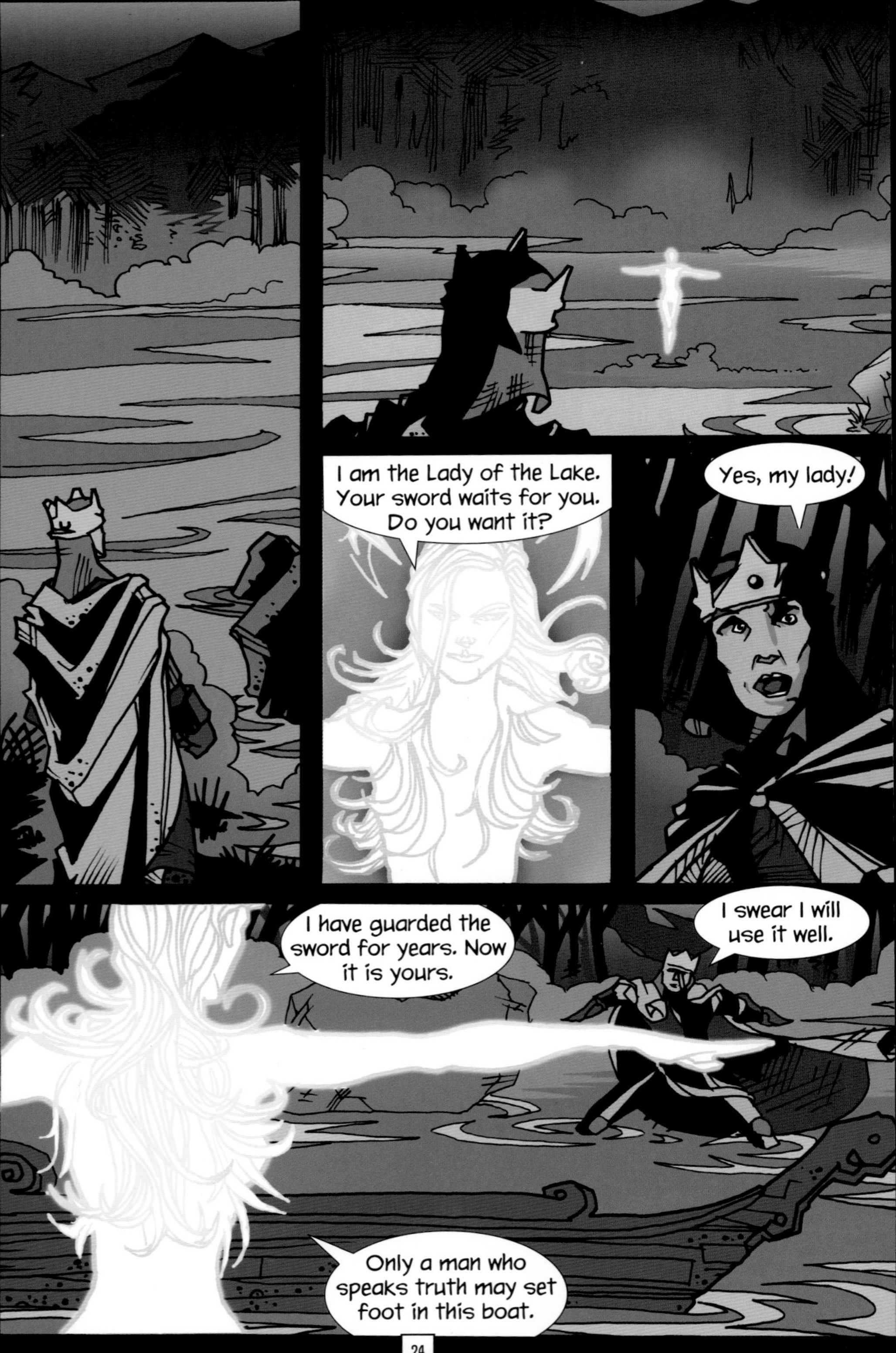
I am the Lady of the Lake. Your sword waits for you. Do you want it?
Yes, my lady!
I have guarded the sword for years. Now it is yours.
I swear I will use it well.
Only a man who speaks truth may set foot in this boat.

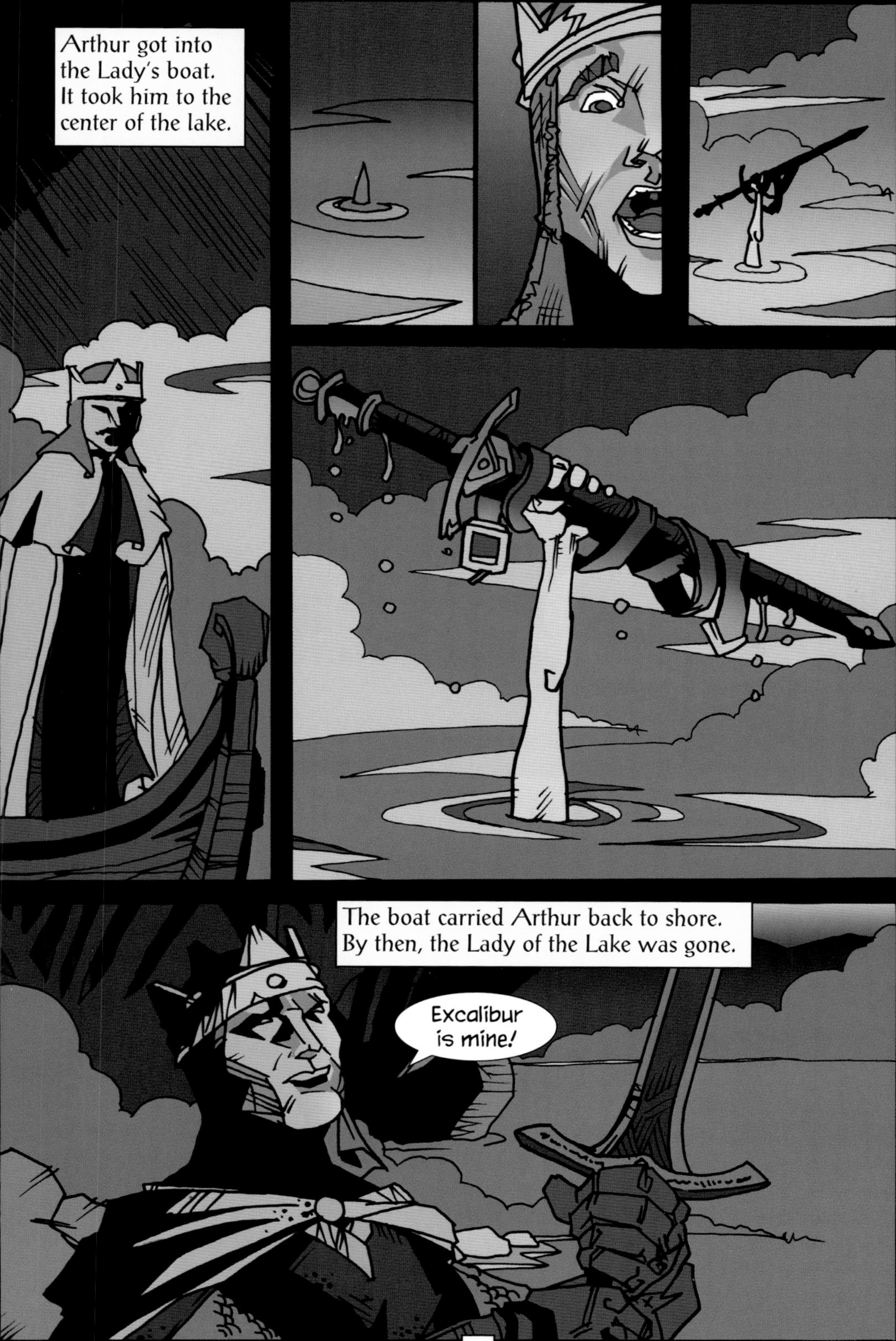
Arthur got into the Lady's boat. It took him to the center of the lake.
The boat carried Arthur back to shore. By then, the Lady of the Lake was gone.
Excalibur is mine!

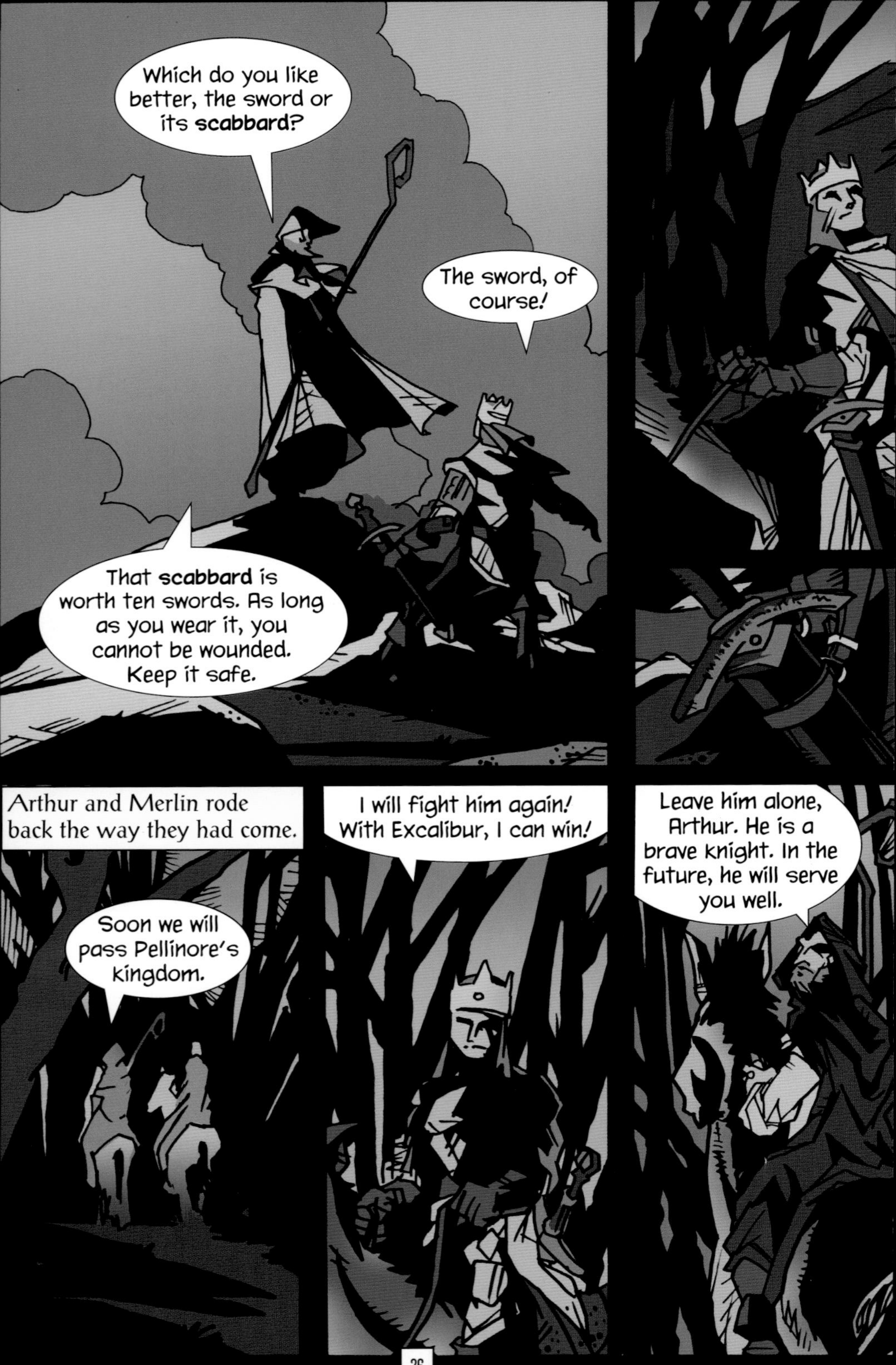
Which do you like better, the sword or its **scabbard**?
The sword, of course!
That **scabbard** is worth ten swords. As long as you wear it, you cannot be wounded. Keep it safe.
Arthur and Merlin rode back the way they had come.
Soon we will pass Pellinore's kingdom.
I will fight him again! With Excalibur, I can win!
Leave him alone, Arthur. He is a brave knight. In the future, he will serve you well.

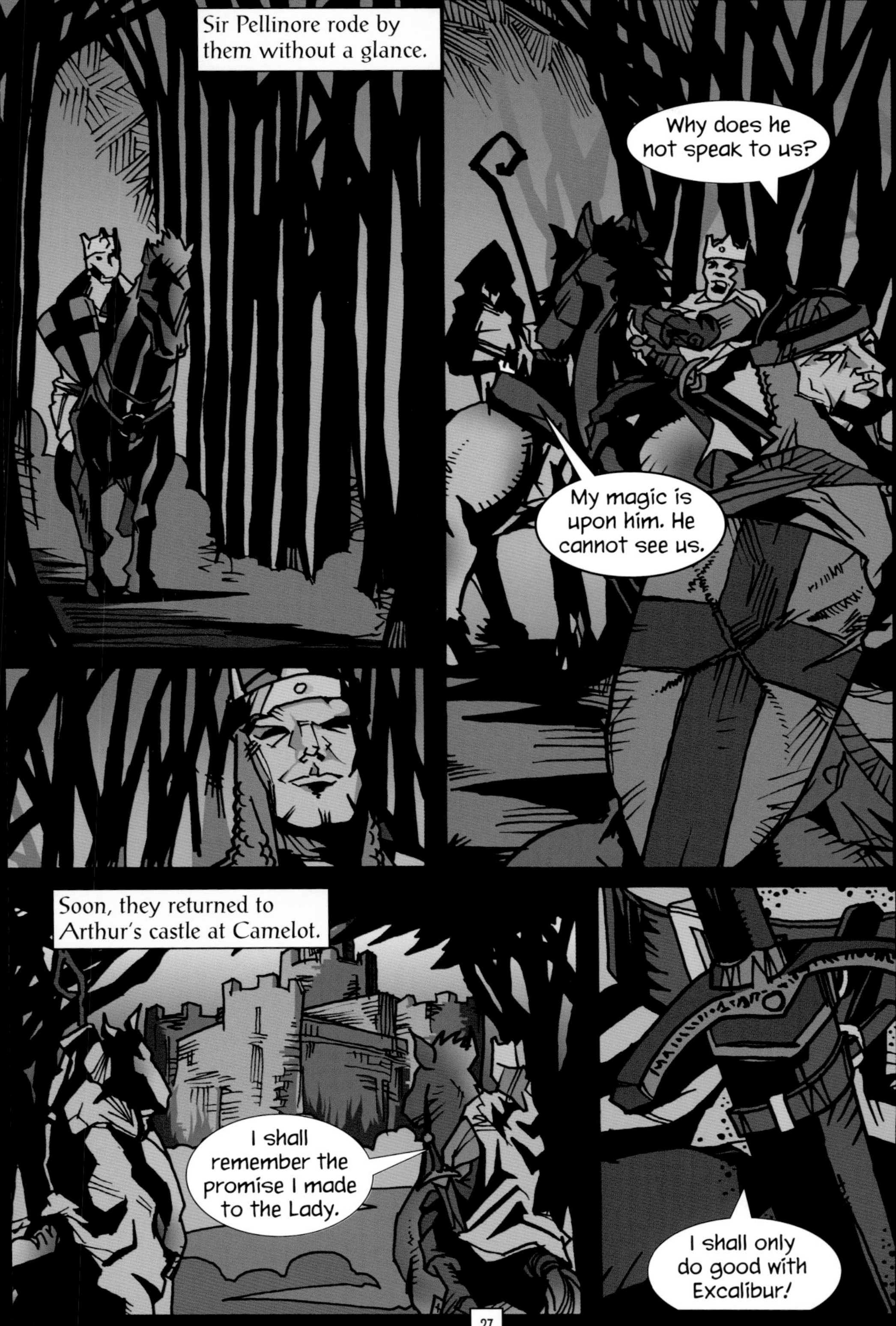

Sir Pellinore rode by them without a glance.
Why does he not speak to us?
My magic is upon him. He cannot see us.
Soon, they returned to Arthur's castle at Camelot.
I shall remember the promise I made to the Lady.
I shall only do good with Excalibur!

Chapter 3

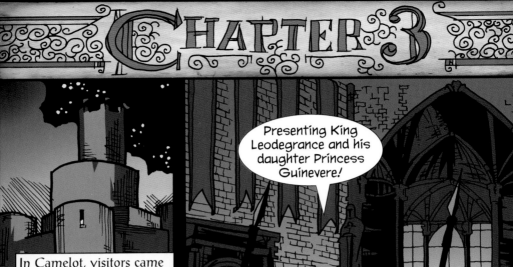

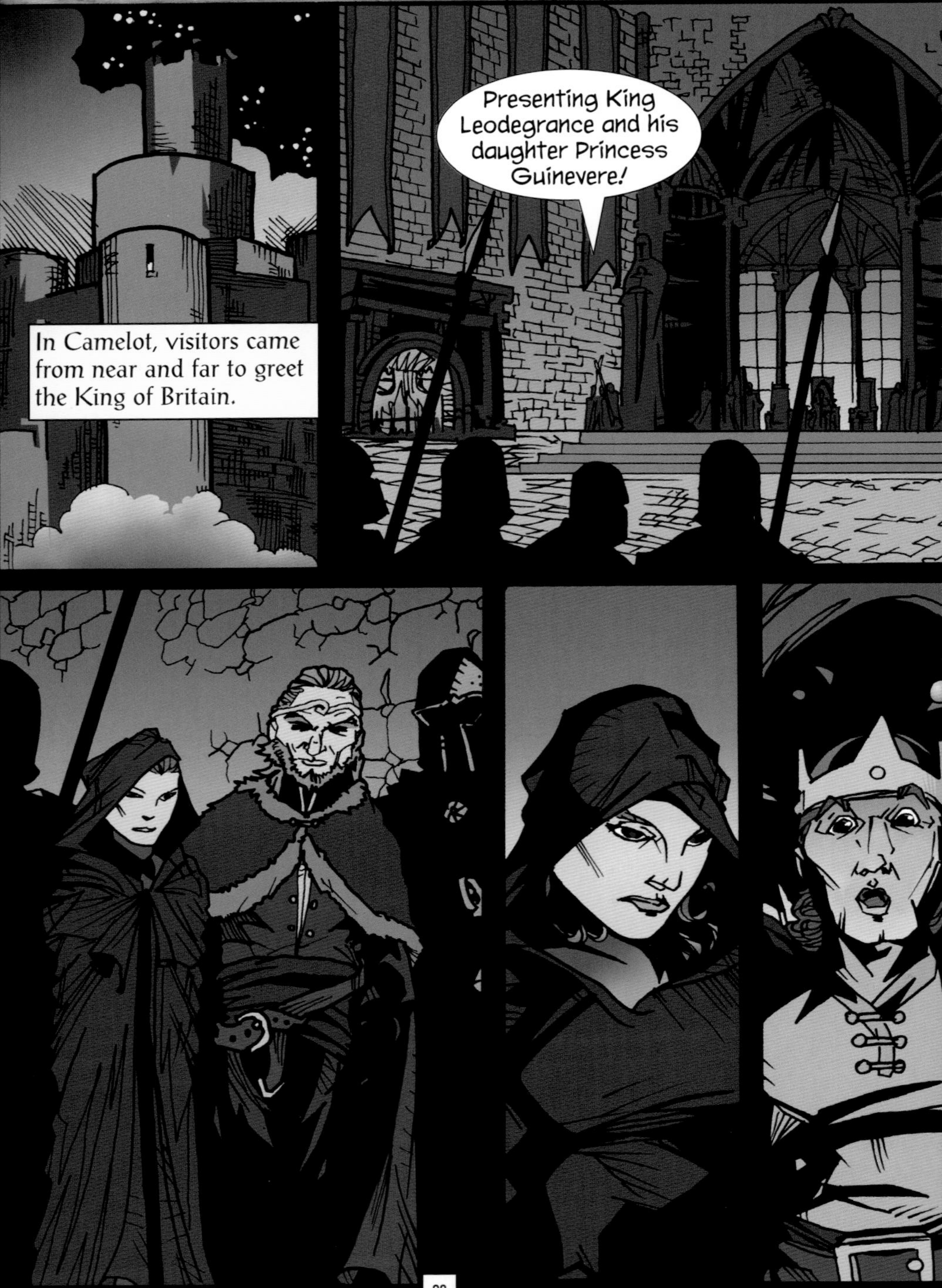
In Camelot, visitors came from near and far to greet the King of Britain.
Presenting King Leodegrance and his daughter Princess Guinevere!

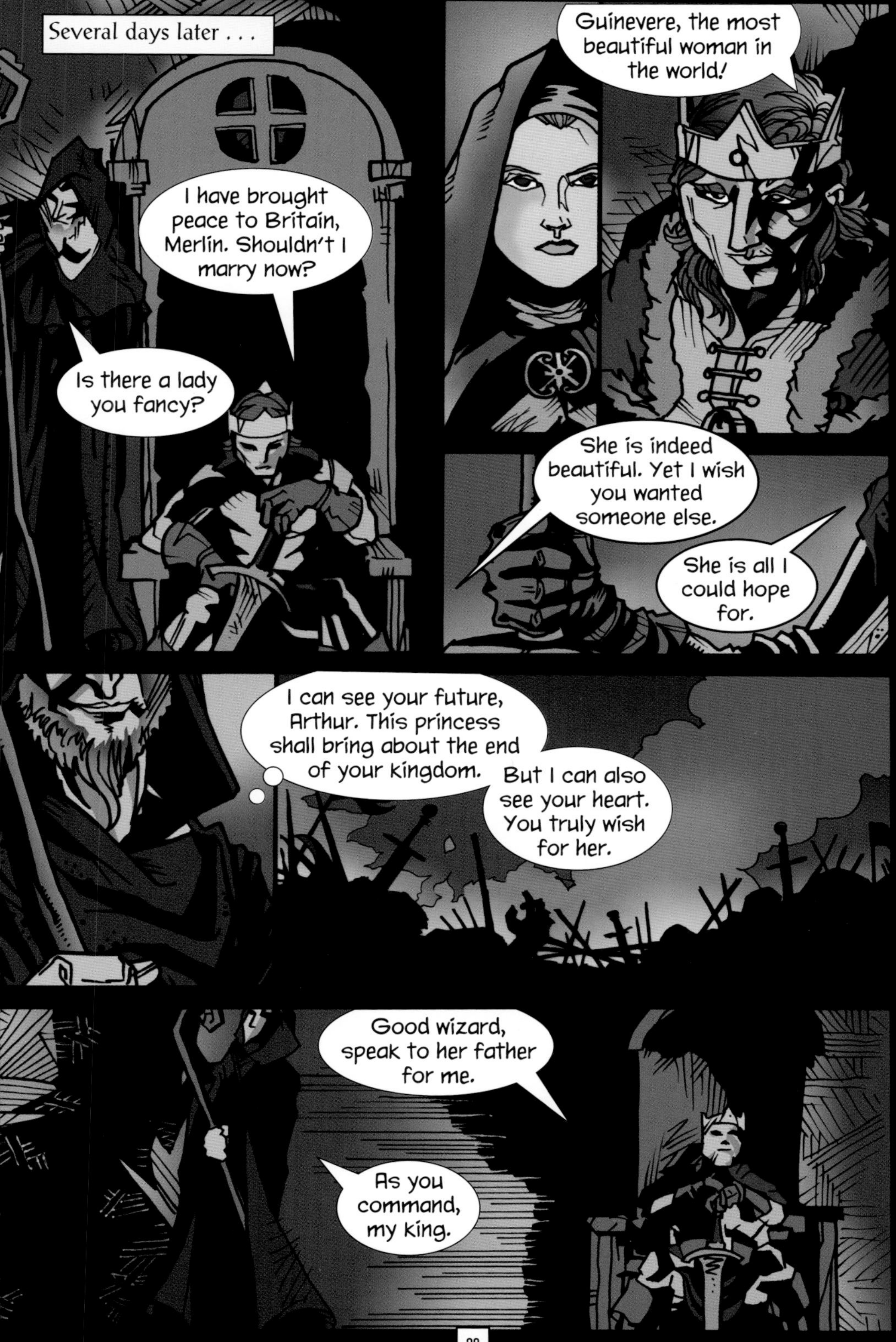
Several days later . . .
I have brought peace to Britain, Merlin. Shouldn't I marry now?
Is there a lady you fancy?
Guinevere, the most beautiful woman in the world!
She is indeed beautiful. Yet I wish you wanted someone else.
She is all I could hope for.
I can see your future, Arthur. This princess shall bring about the end of your kingdom.
But I can also see your heart. You truly wish for her.
Good wizard, speak to her father for me.
As you command, my king.

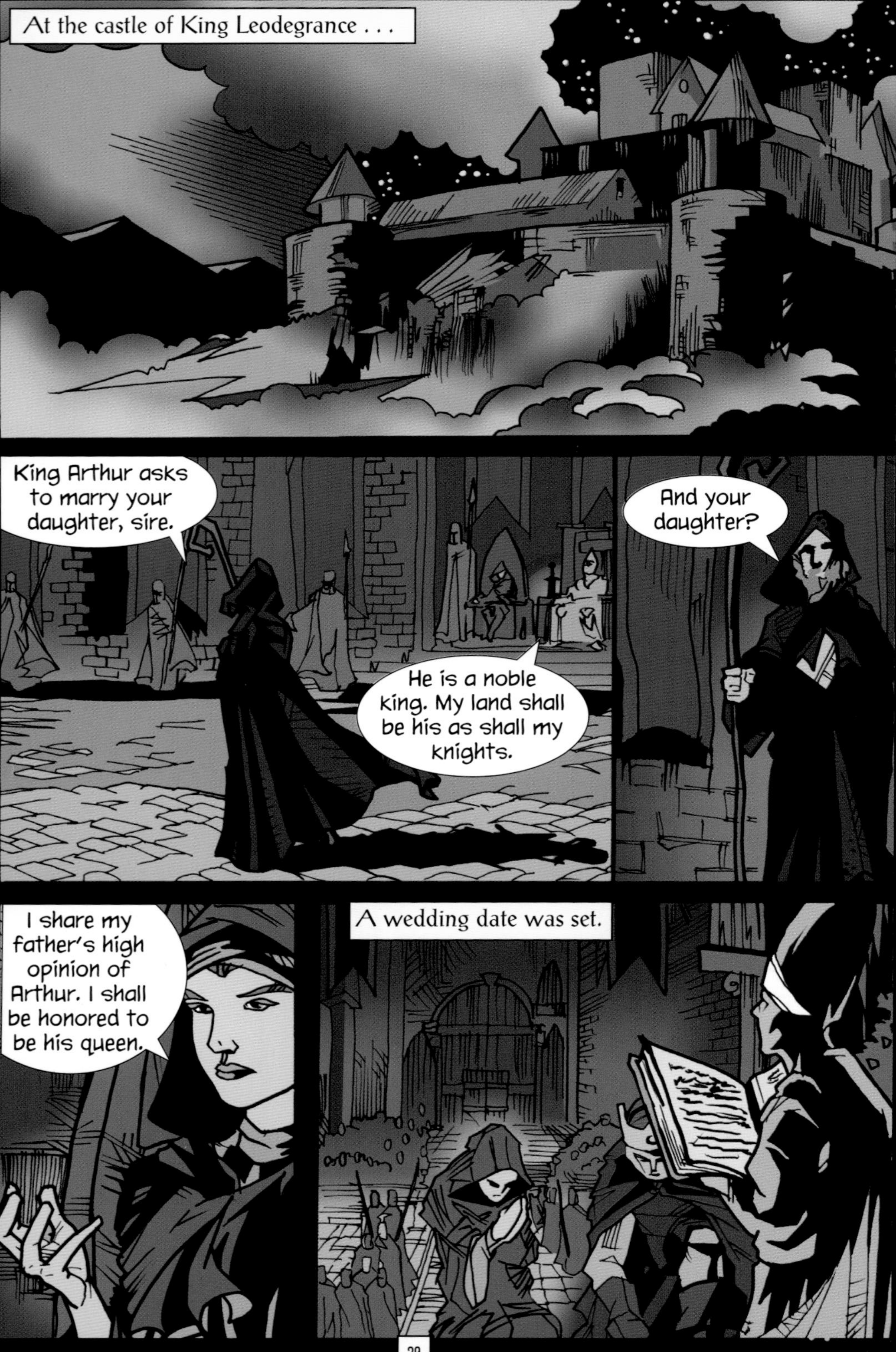
At the castle of King Leodegrance . . .
King Arthur asks to marry your daughter, sire.
He is a noble king. My land shall be his as shall my knights.
And your daughter?
I share my father's high opinion of Arthur. I shall be honored to be his queen.
A wedding date was set.

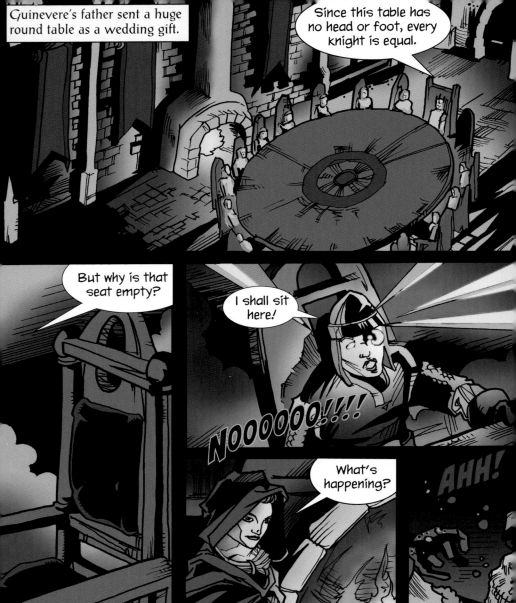

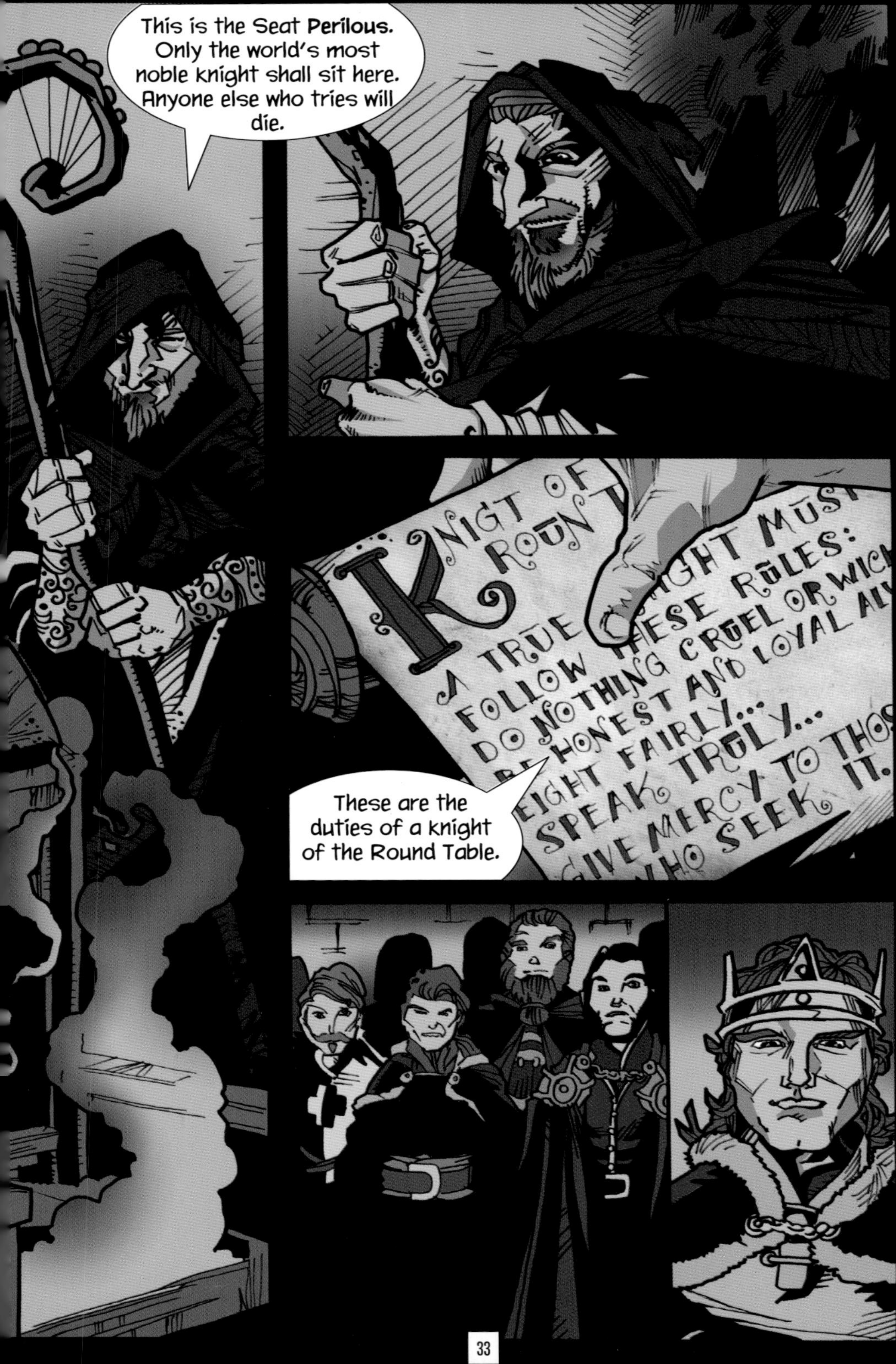
This is the Seat Perilous. Only the world's most noble knight shall sit here. Anyone else who tries will die.
These are the duties of a knight of the Round Table.

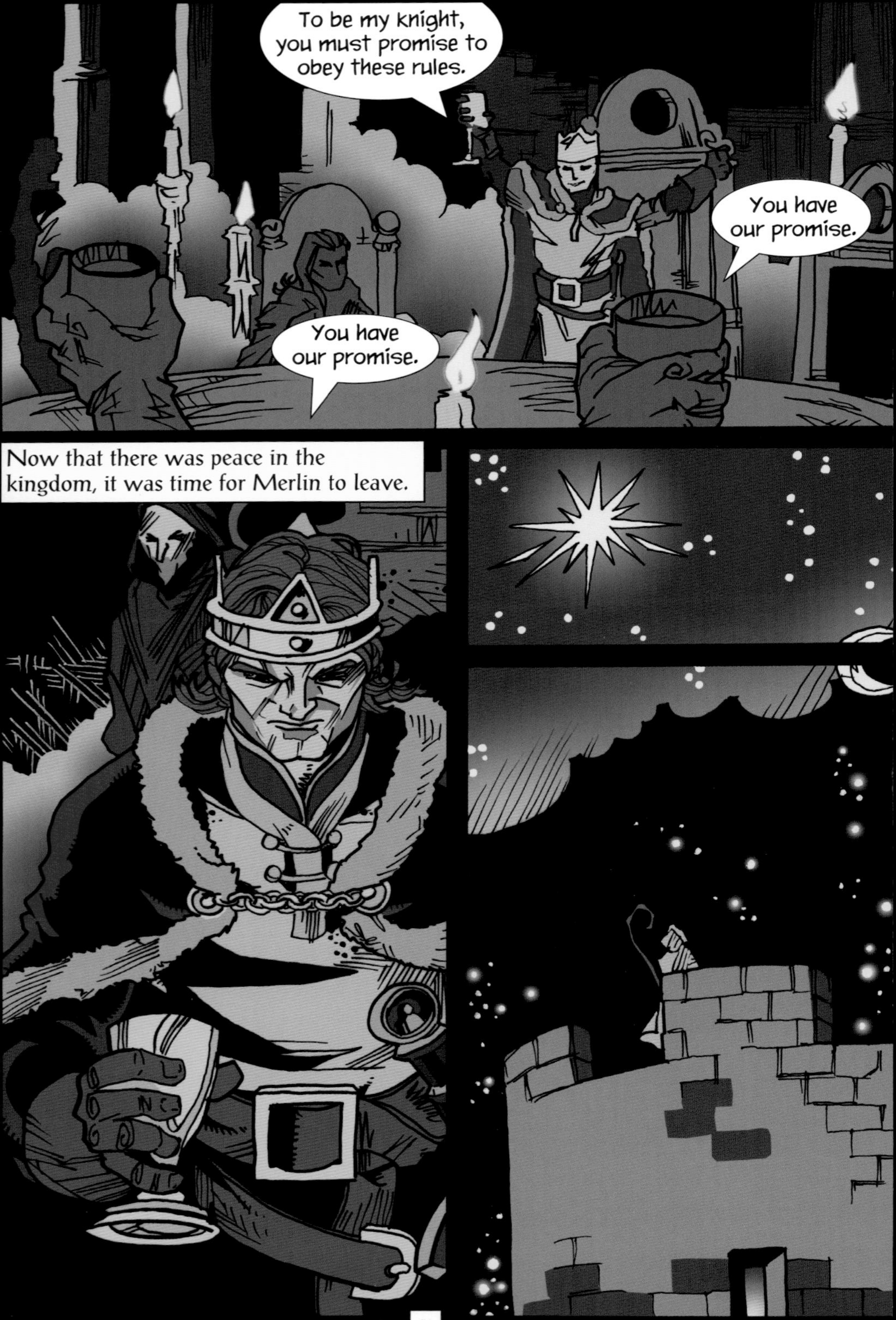
To be my knight, you must promise to obey these rules.
You have our promise.
You have our promise.
Now that there was peace in the kingdom, it was time for Merlin to leave.

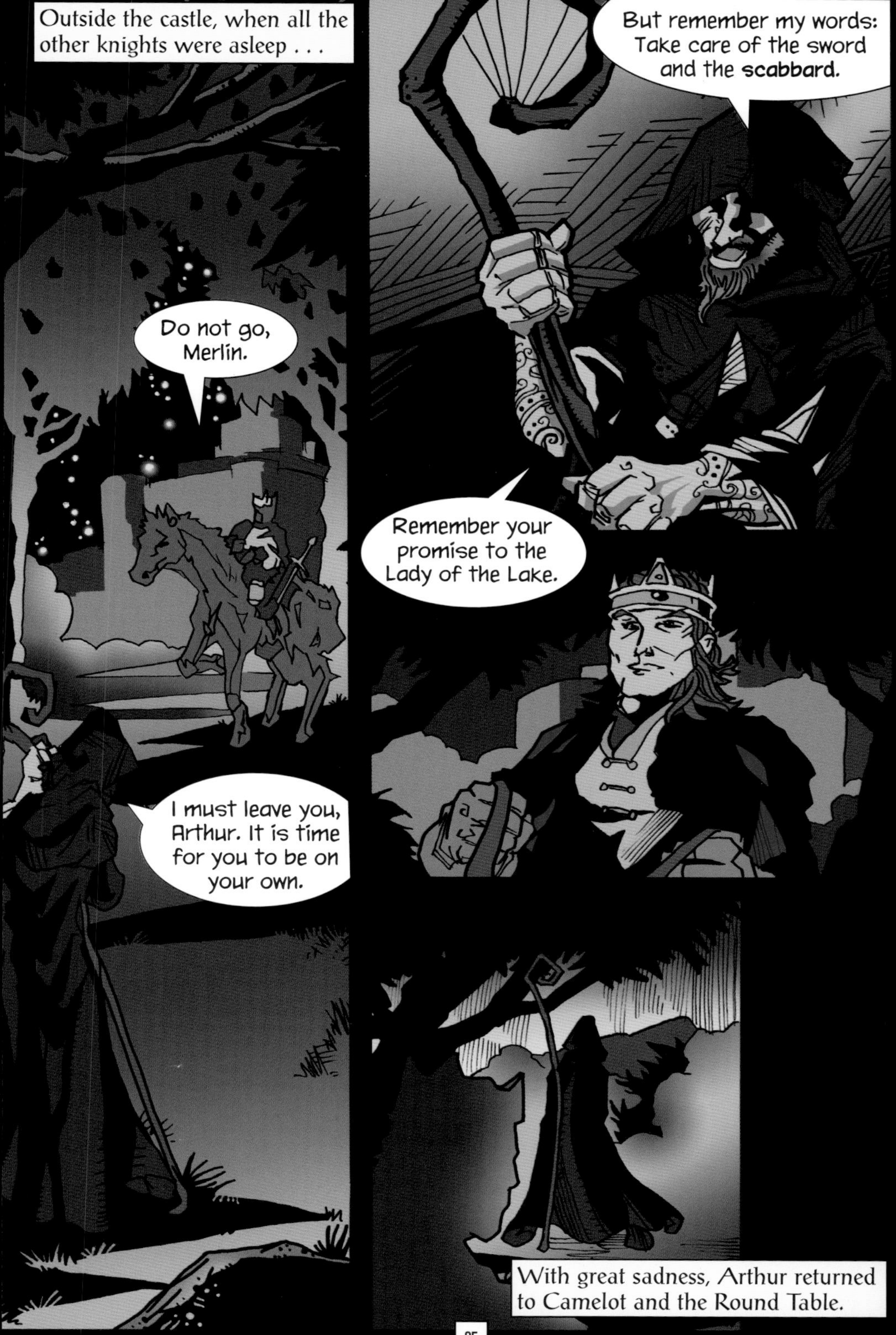
Outside the castle, when all the other knights were asleep . . .
Do not go, Merlin.
I must leave you, Arthur. It is time for you to be on your own.
But remember my words: Take care of the sword and the **scabbard.**
Remember your promise to the Lady of the Lake.
With great sadness, Arthur returned to Camelot and the Round Table.

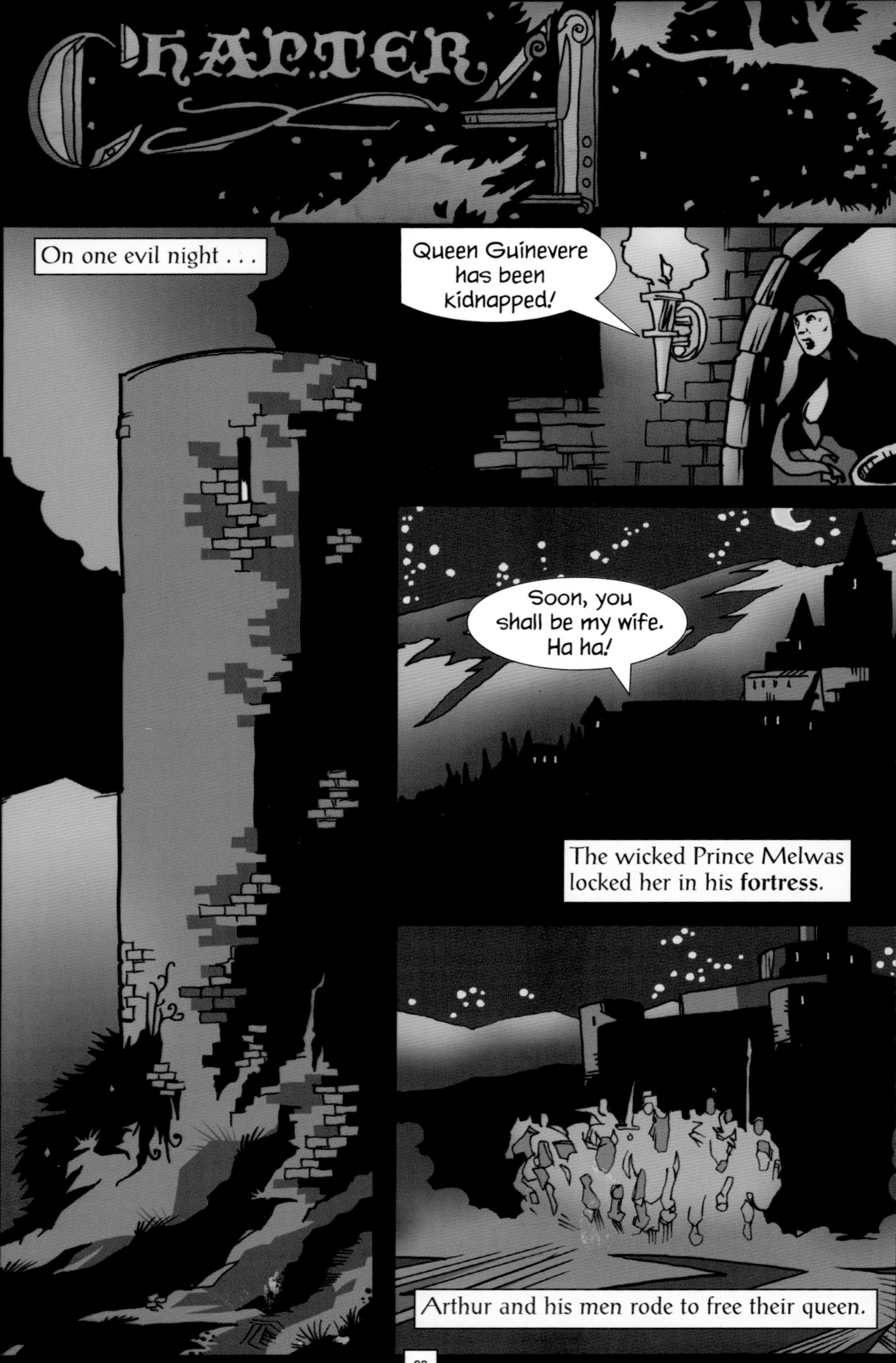
Chapter 4
On one evil night . . .
Queen Guinevere has been kidnapped!
Soon, you shall be my wife. Ha ha!
The wicked Prince Melwas locked her in his **fortress**.
Arthur and his men rode to free their queen.

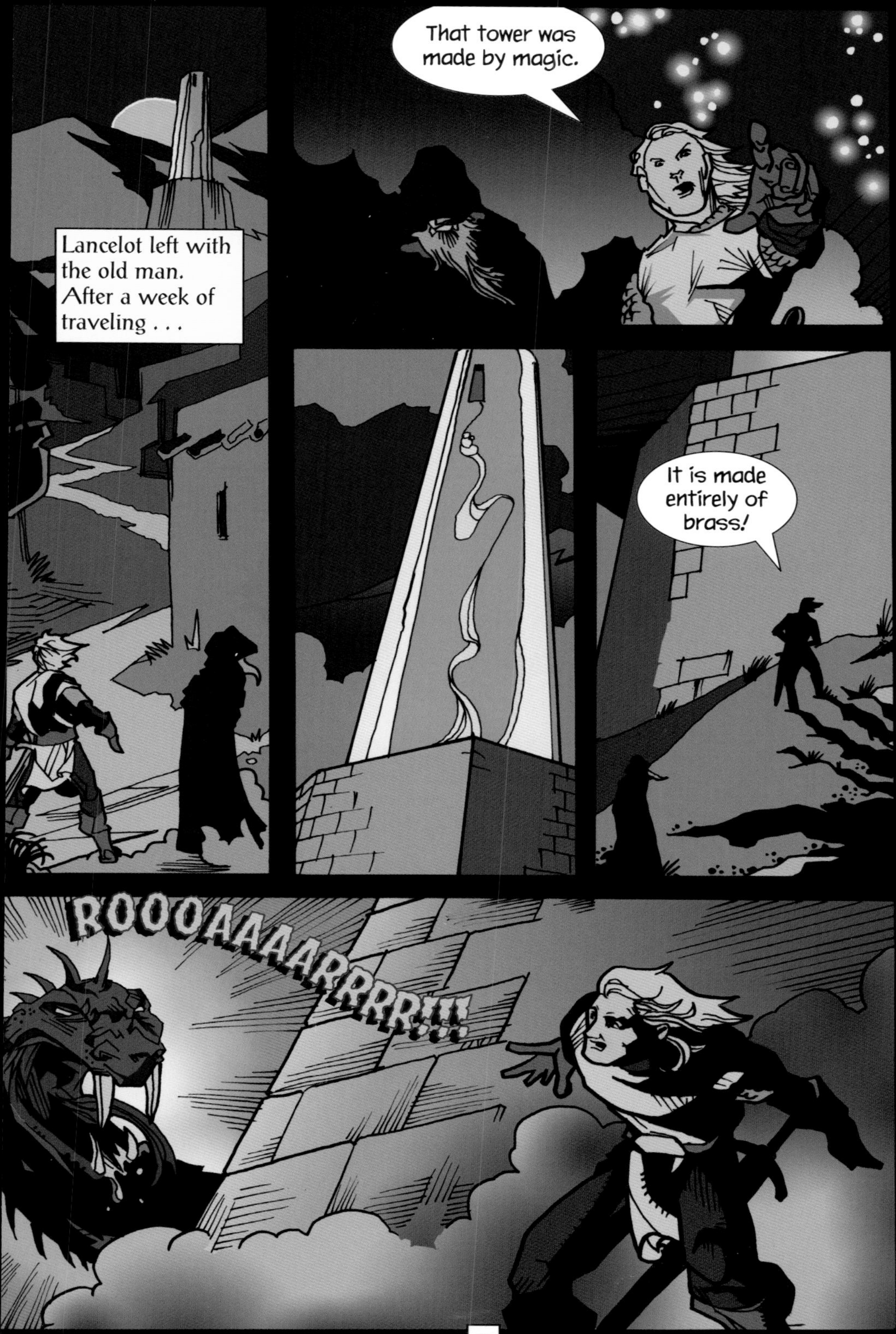
Lancelot left with the old man. After a week of traveling . . .
That tower was made by magic.
It is made entirely of brass!
ROOOAAAAARRRRR!!!

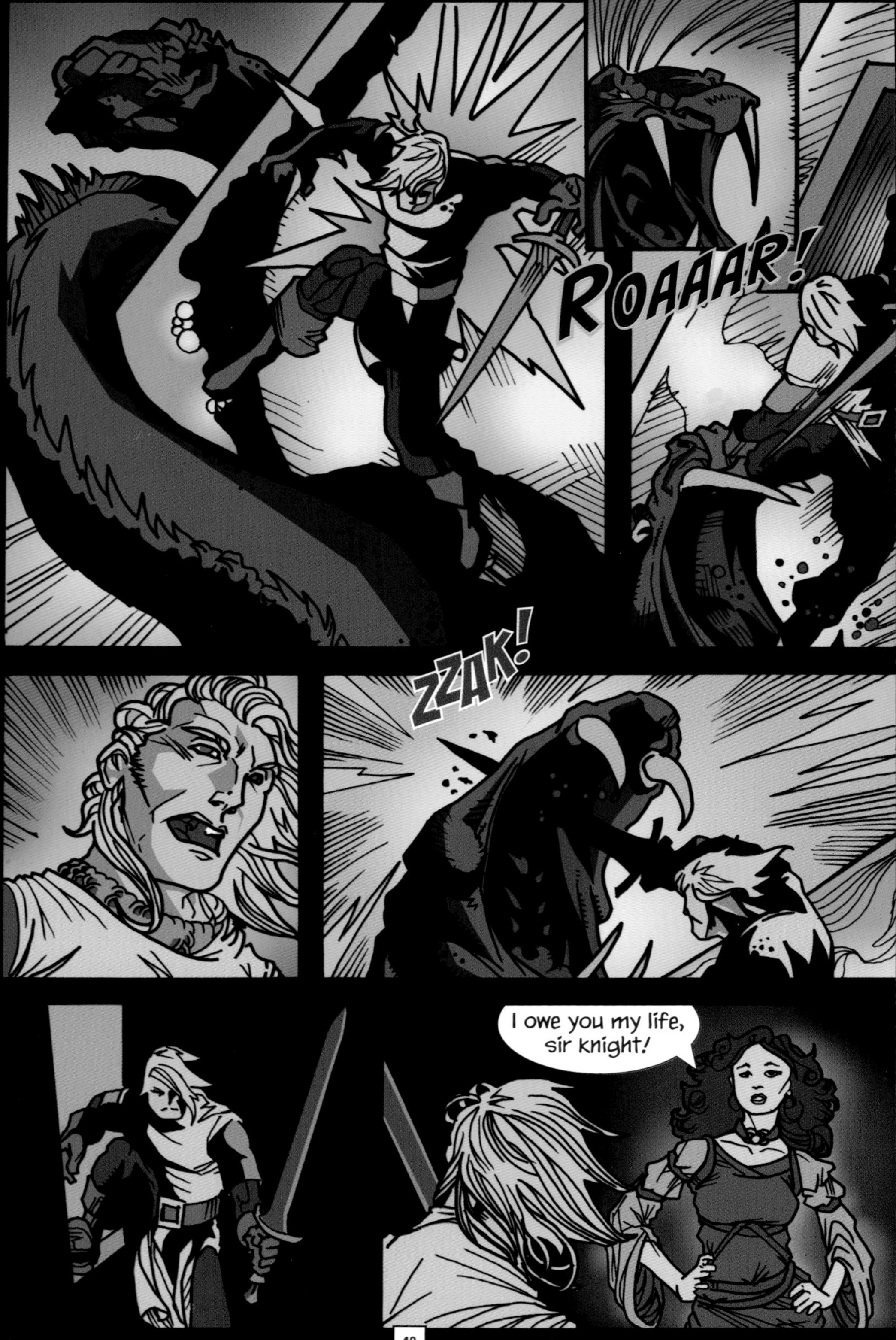
ROAAAR!
ZZAK!
I owe you my life, sir knight!

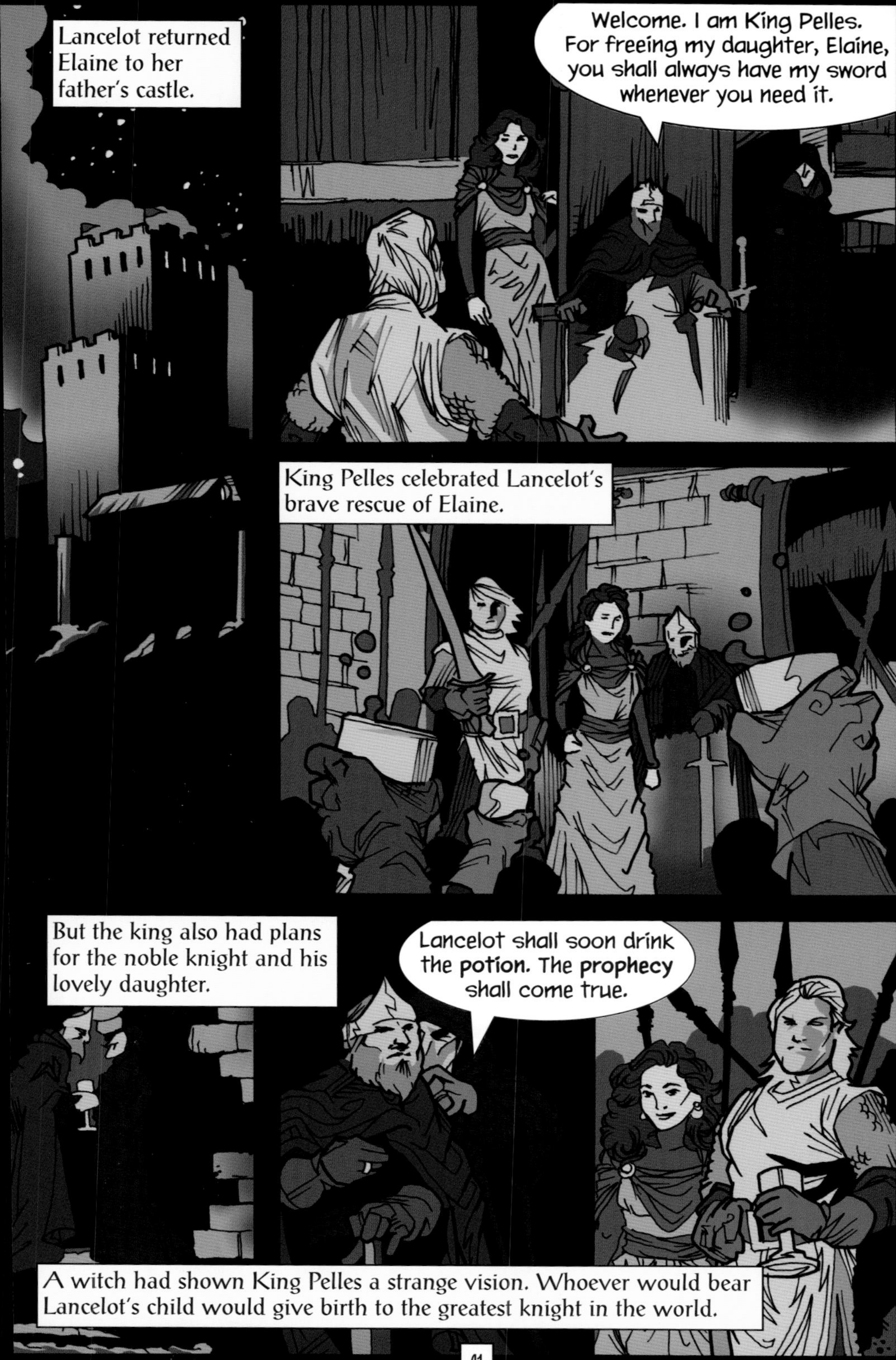
Lancelot returned Elaine to her father's castle.
Welcome. I am King Pelles. For freeing my daughter, Elaine, you shall always have my sword whenever you need it.
King Pelles celebrated Lancelot's brave rescue of Elaine.
But the king also had plans for the noble knight and his lovely daughter.
Lancelot shall soon drink the **potion.** The **prophecy** shall come true.
A witch had shown King Pelles a strange vision. Whoever would bear Lancelot's child would give birth to the greatest knight in the world.

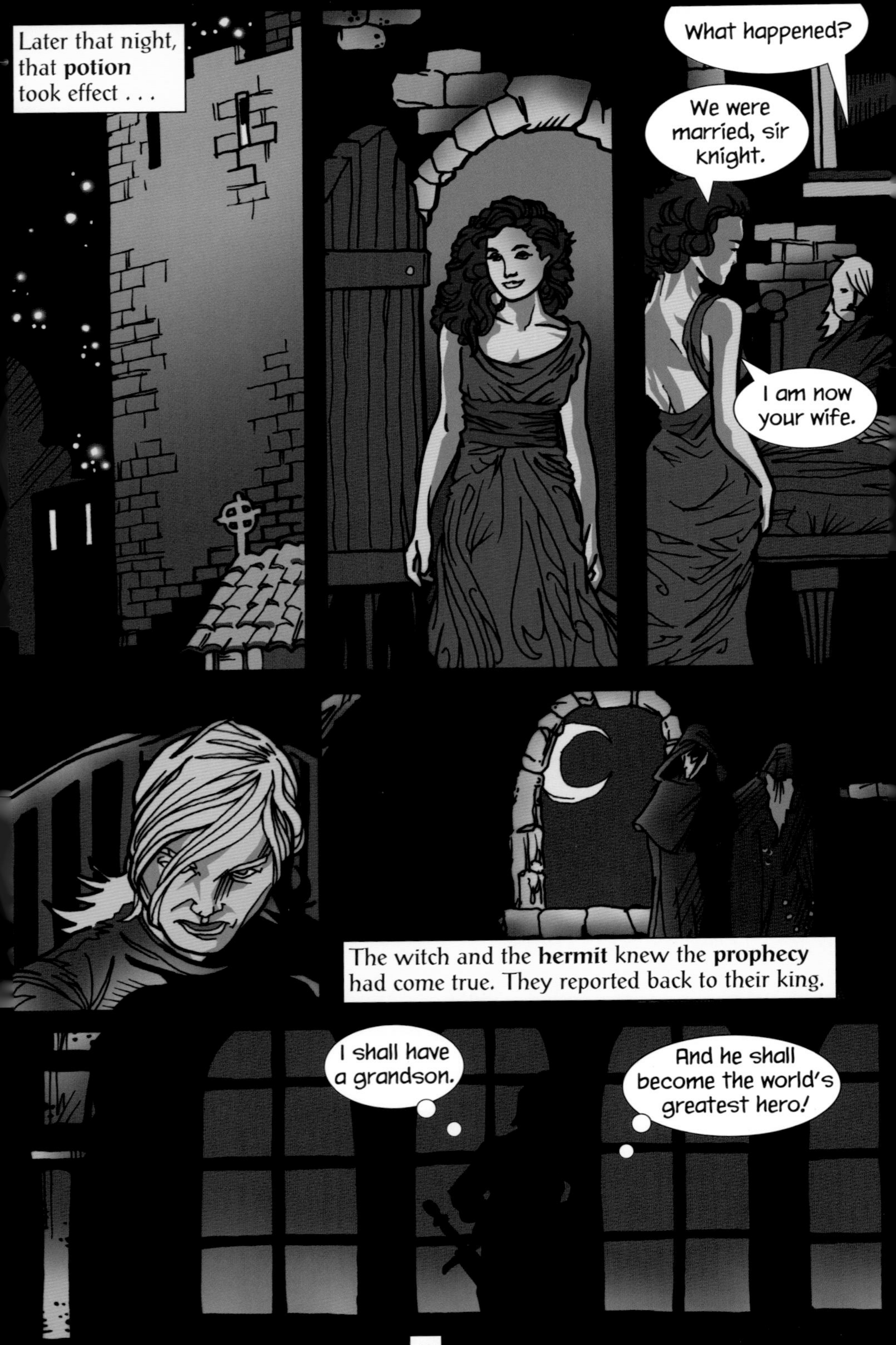

Later that night, that **potion** took effect . . .
What happened?
We were married, sir knight.
I am now your wife.
The witch and the **hermit** knew the **prophecy** had come true. They reported back to their king.
I shall have a grandson.
And he shall become the world's greatest hero!

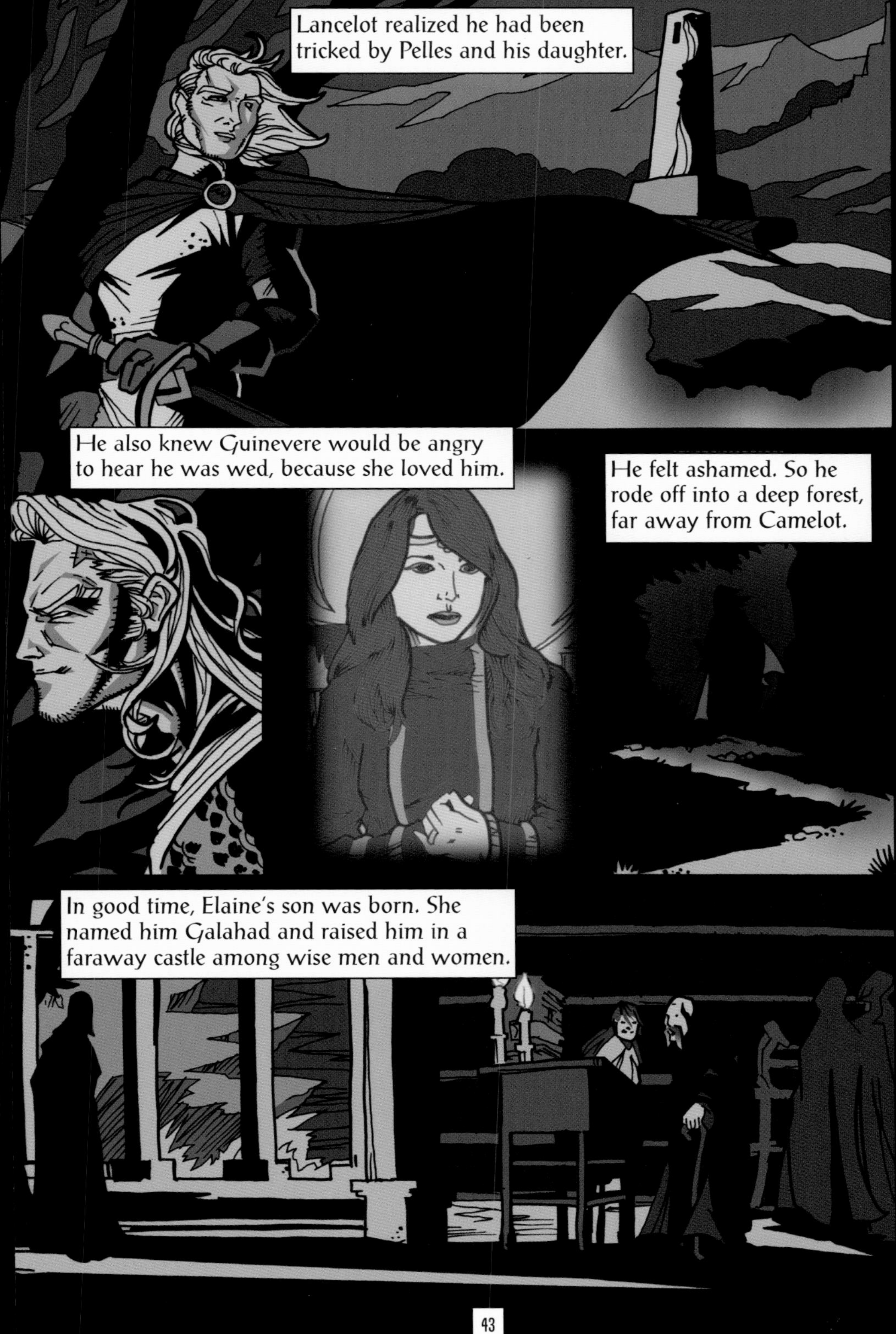
Lancelot realized he had been tricked by Pelles and his daughter.
He also knew Guinevere would be angry to hear he was wed, because she loved him.
He felt ashamed. So he rode off into a deep forest, far away from Camelot.
In good time, Elaine's son was born. She named him Galahad and raised him in a faraway castle among wise men and women.

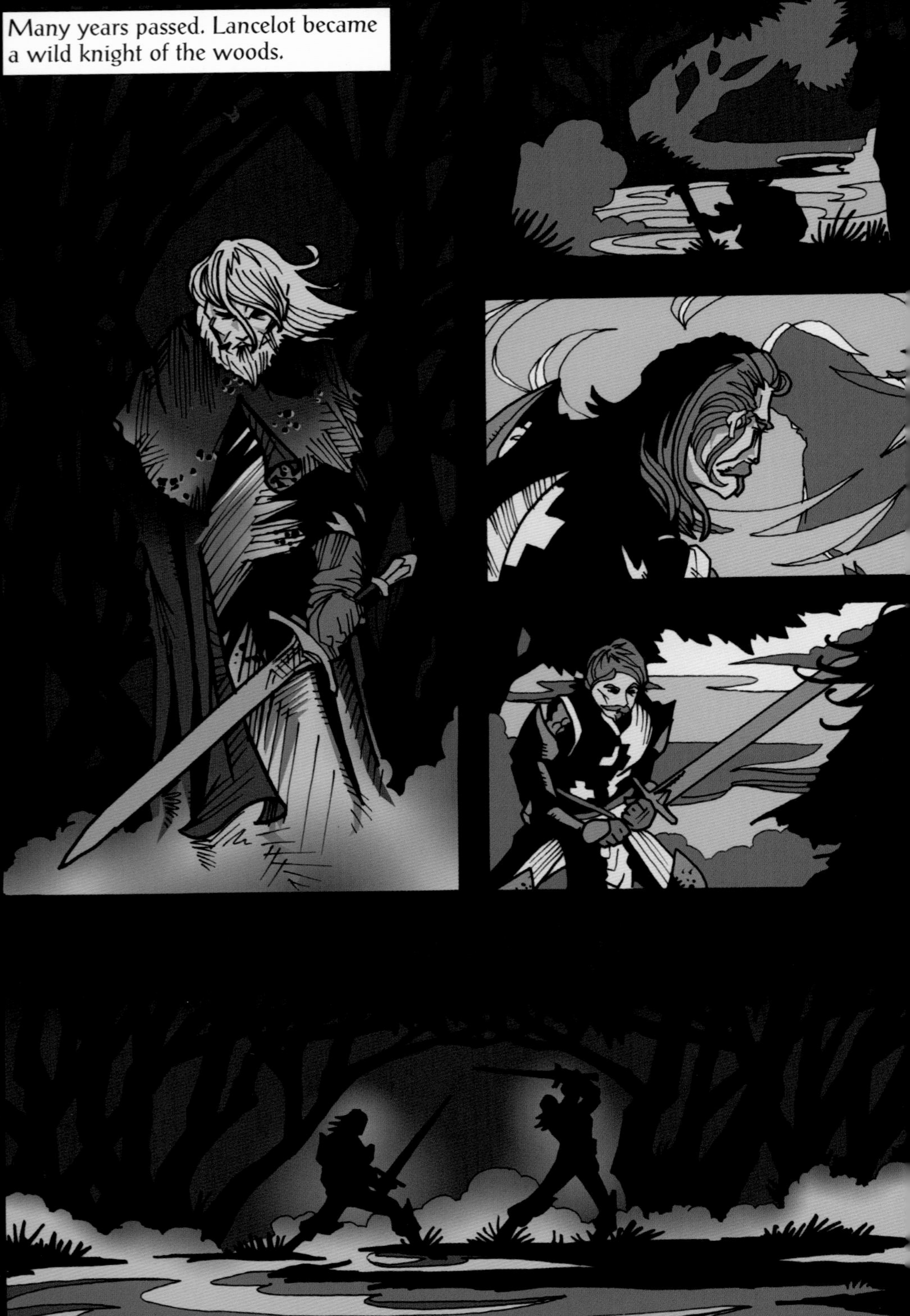
Many years passed. Lancelot became a wild knight of the woods.

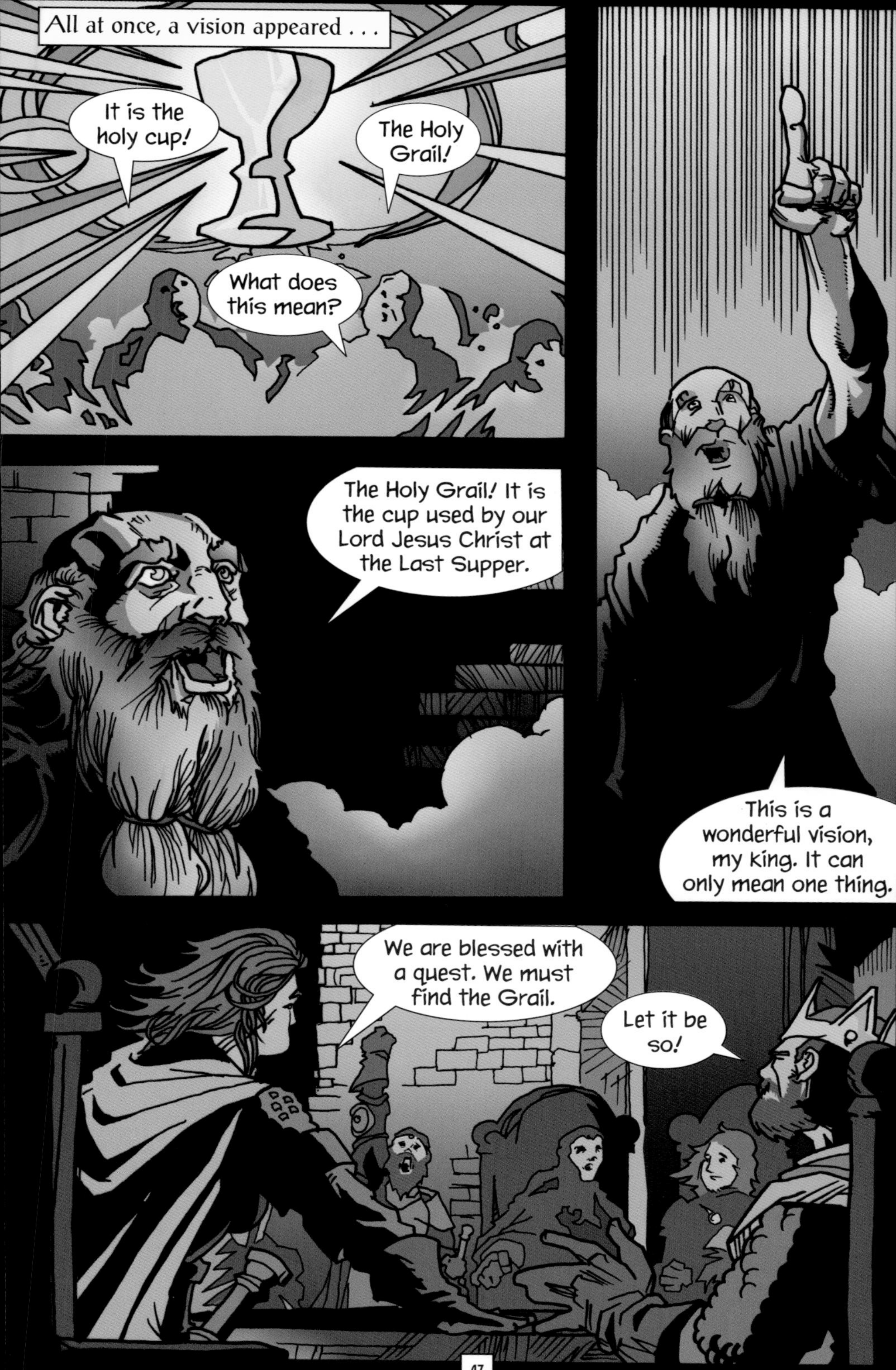
All at once, a vision appeared . . .
It is the holy cup!
The Holy Grail!
What does this mean?
The Holy Grail! It is the cup used by our Lord Jesus Christ at the Last Supper.
This is a wonderful vision, my king. It can only mean one thing.
We are blessed with a quest. We must find the Grail.
Let it be so!

Arthur's knights passed through many adventures as they searched for the Holy Grail.

Finally, three of Arthur's knights – Galahad, Percival, and Bors – came to a ruined castle.

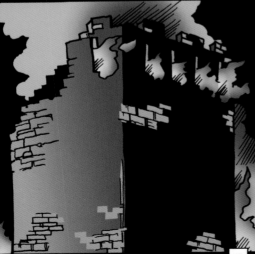

Look! It is Lancelot.

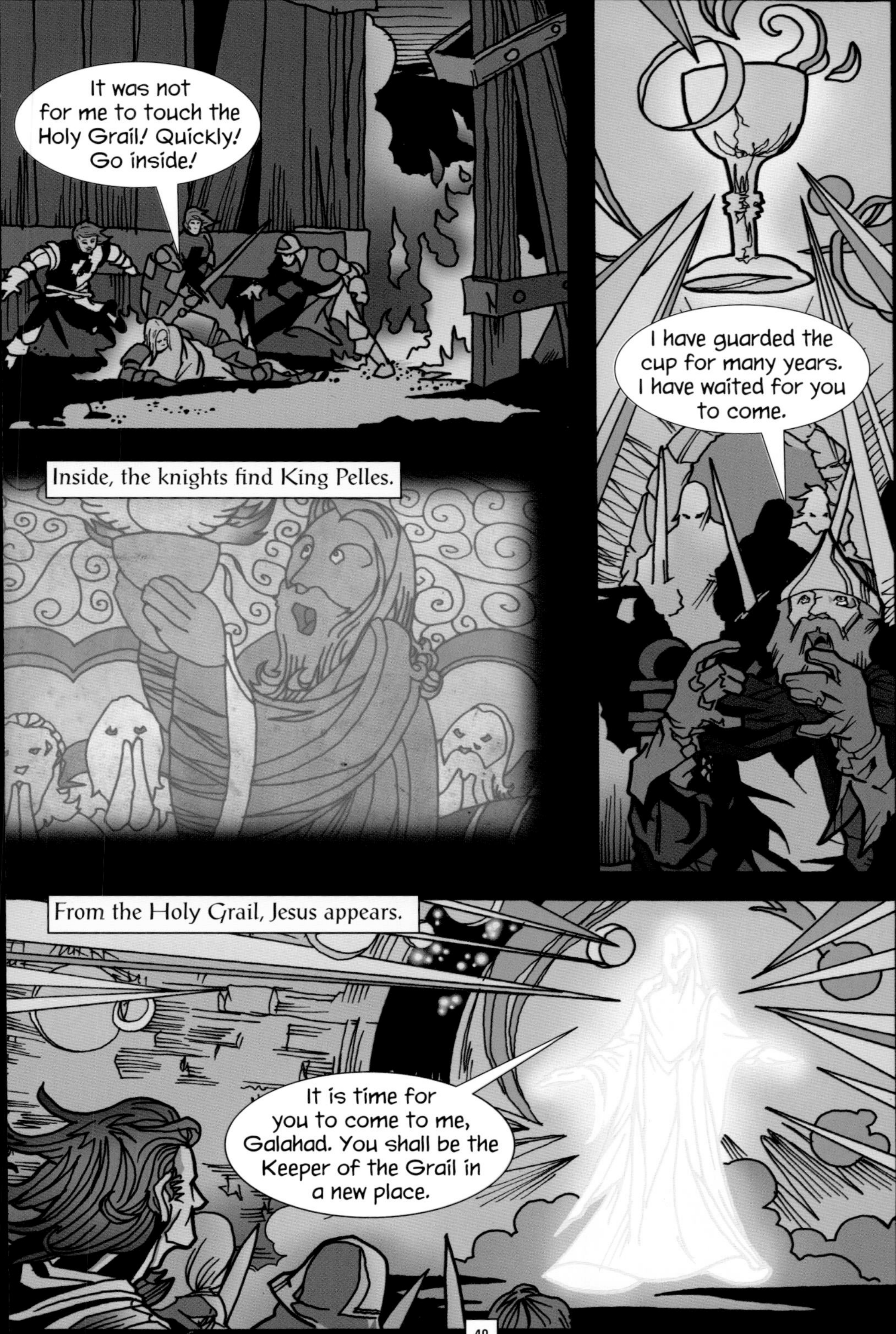

It was not for me to touch the Holy Grail! Quickly! Go inside!
I have guarded the cup for many years. I have waited for you to come.
Inside, the knights find King Pelles.
From the Holy Grail, Jesus appears.
It is time for you to come to me, Galahad. You shall be the Keeper of the Grail in a new place.

Galahad drank from the cup, and then . . .

Galahad and the Grail were never seen again.

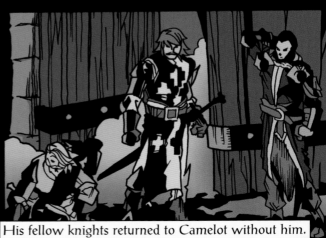

His fellow knights returned to Camelot without him.

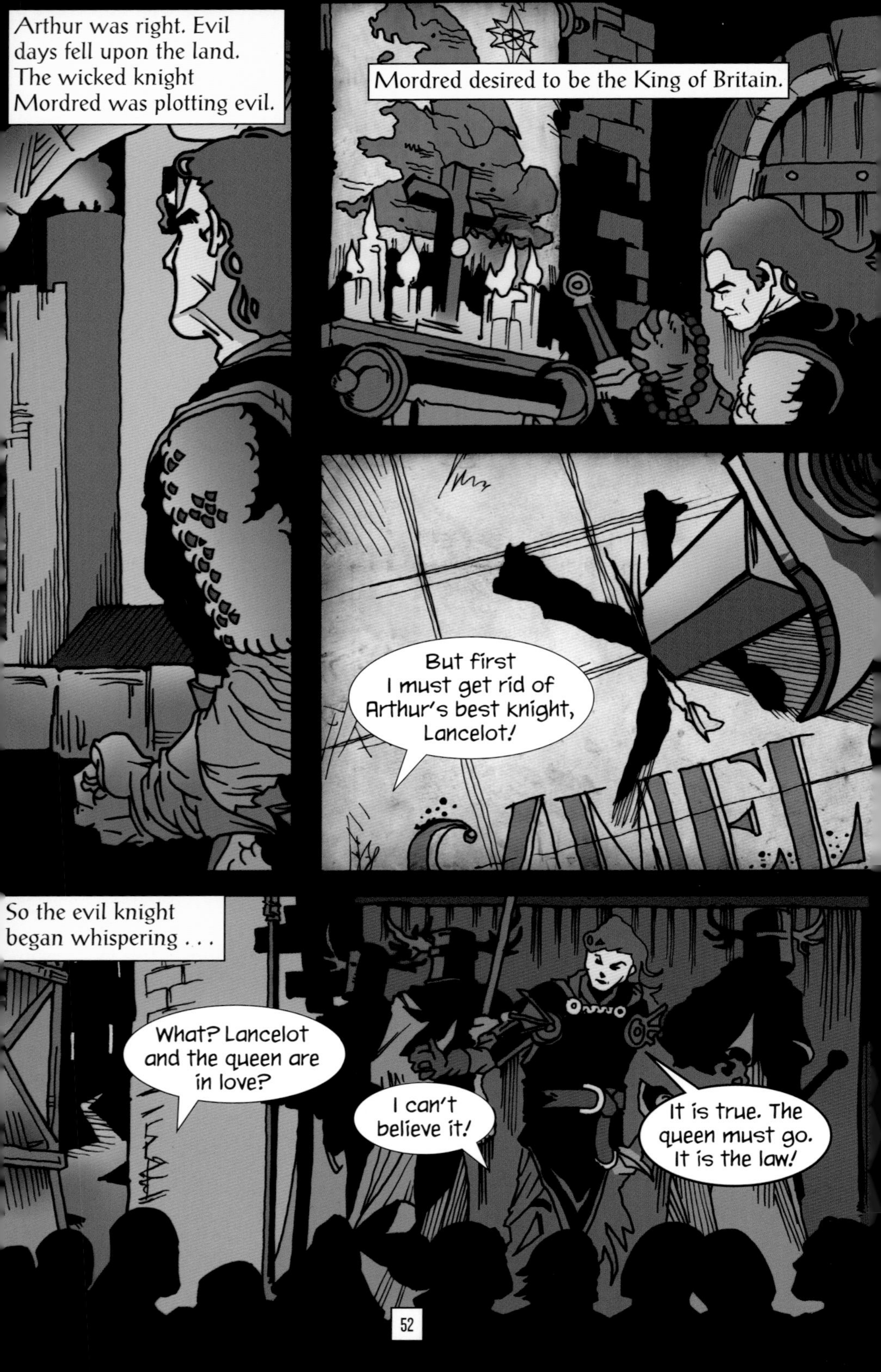
Arthur was right. Evil days fell upon the land. The wicked knight Mordred was plotting evil.
Mordred desired to be the King of Britain.
But first I must get rid of Arthur's best knight, Lancelot!
So the evil knight began whispering . . .
What? Lancelot and the queen are in love?
I can't believe it!
It is true. The queen must go. It is the law!

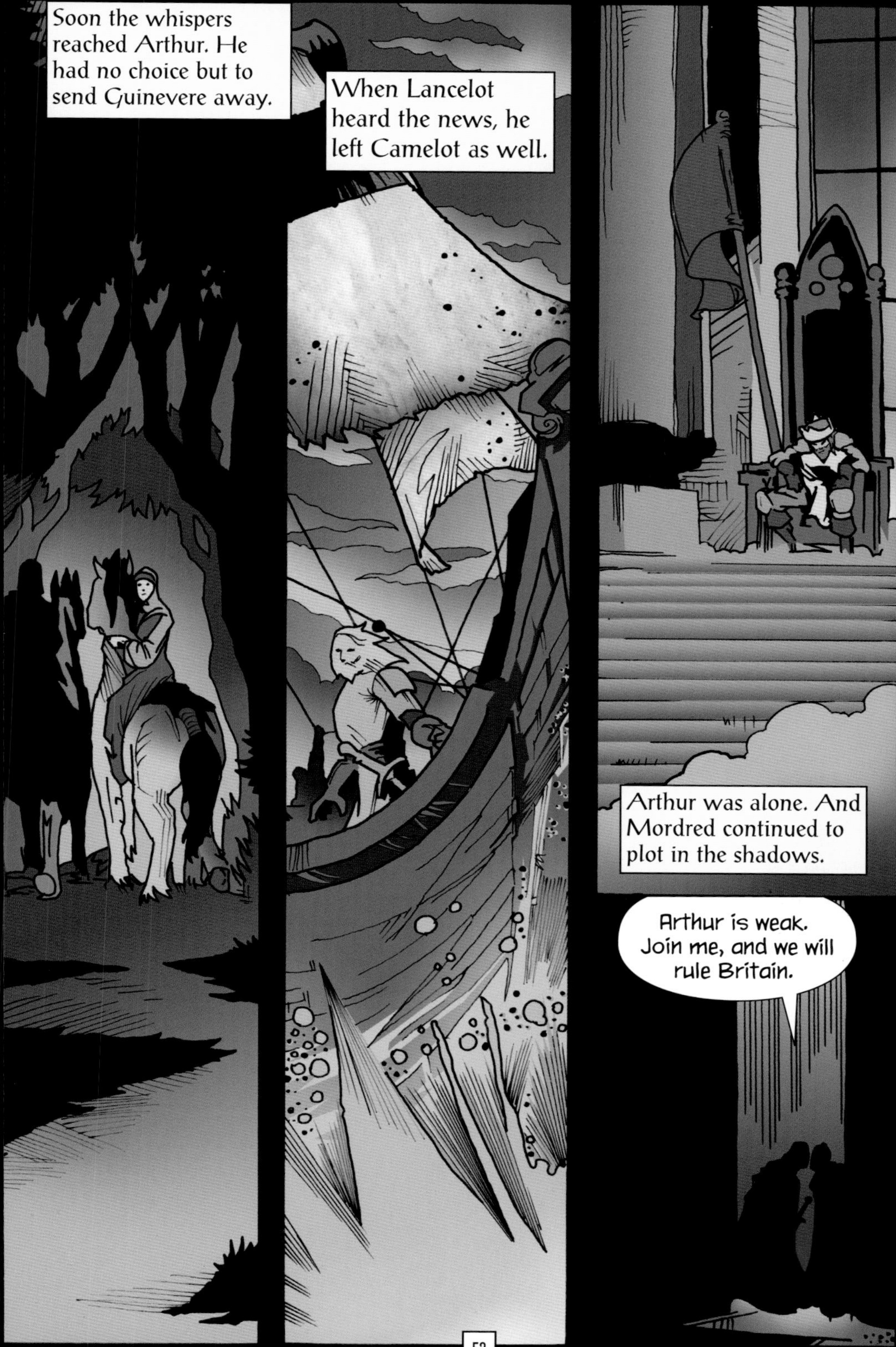
Soon the whispers reached Arthur. He had no choice but to send Guinevere away.
When Lancelot heard the news, he left Camelot as well.
Arthur was alone. And Mordred continued to plot in the shadows.
Arthur is weak. Join me, and we will rule Britain.

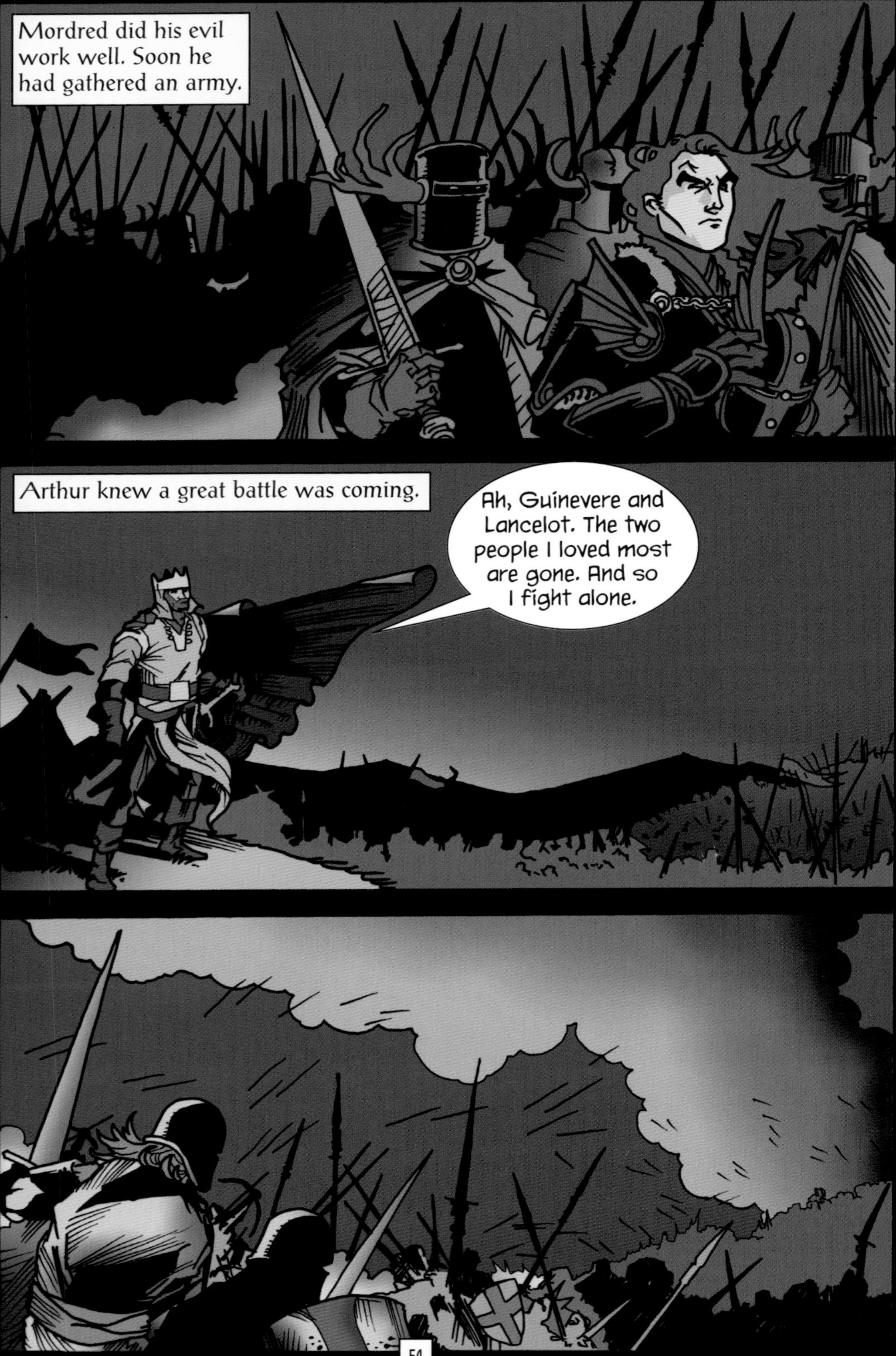
Mordred did his evil work well. Soon he had gathered an army.
Arthur knew a great battle was coming.
Ah, Guinevere and Lancelot. The two people I loved most are gone. And so I fight alone.

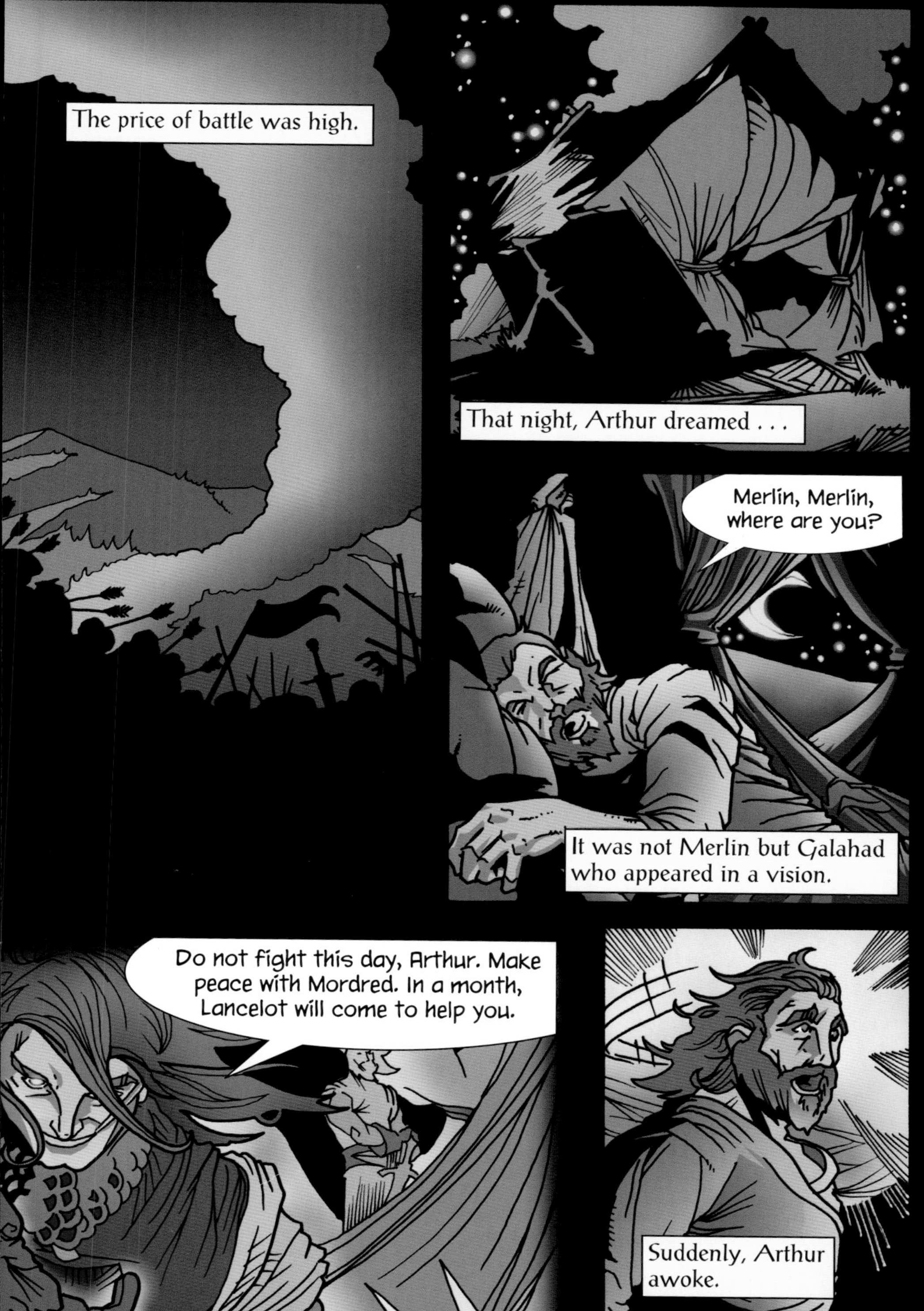
The price of battle was high.
That night, Arthur dreamed . . .
Merlin, Merlin, where are you?
It was not Merlin but Galahad who appeared in a vision.
Do not fight this day, Arthur. Make peace with Mordred. In a month, Lancelot will come to help you.
Suddenly, Arthur awoke.

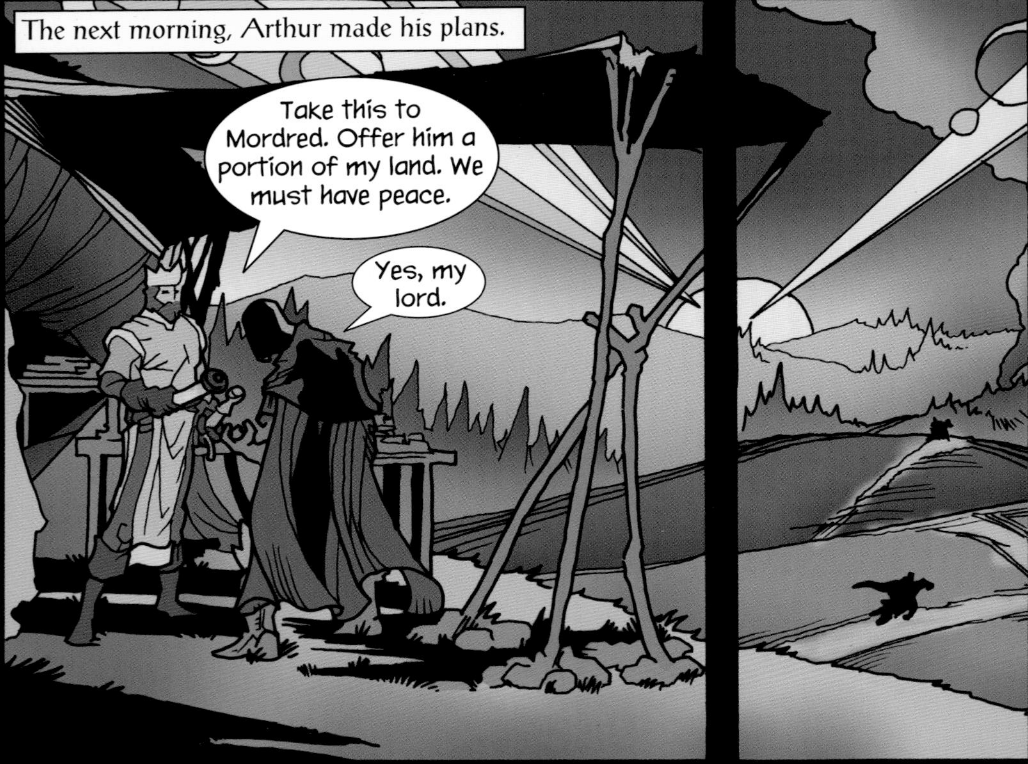
The next morning, Arthur made his plans.
Take this to Mordred. Offer him a portion of my land. We must have peace.
Yes, my lord.

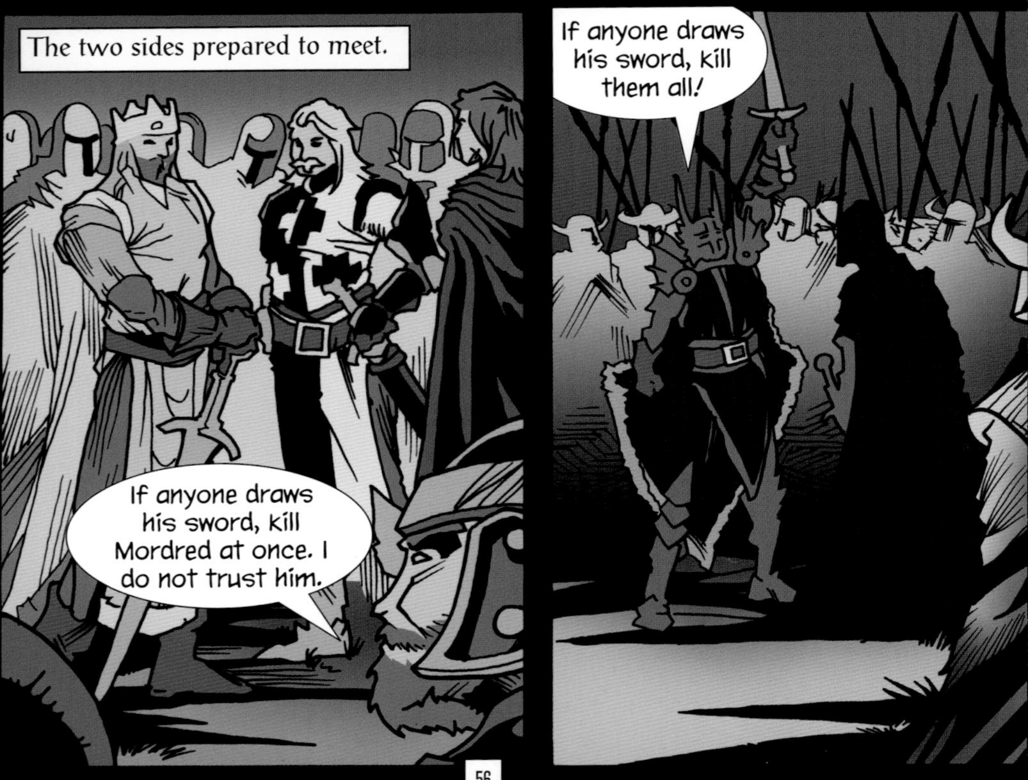
The two sides prepared to meet.
If anyone draws his sword, kill Mordred at once. I do not trust him.
If anyone draws his sword, kill them all!

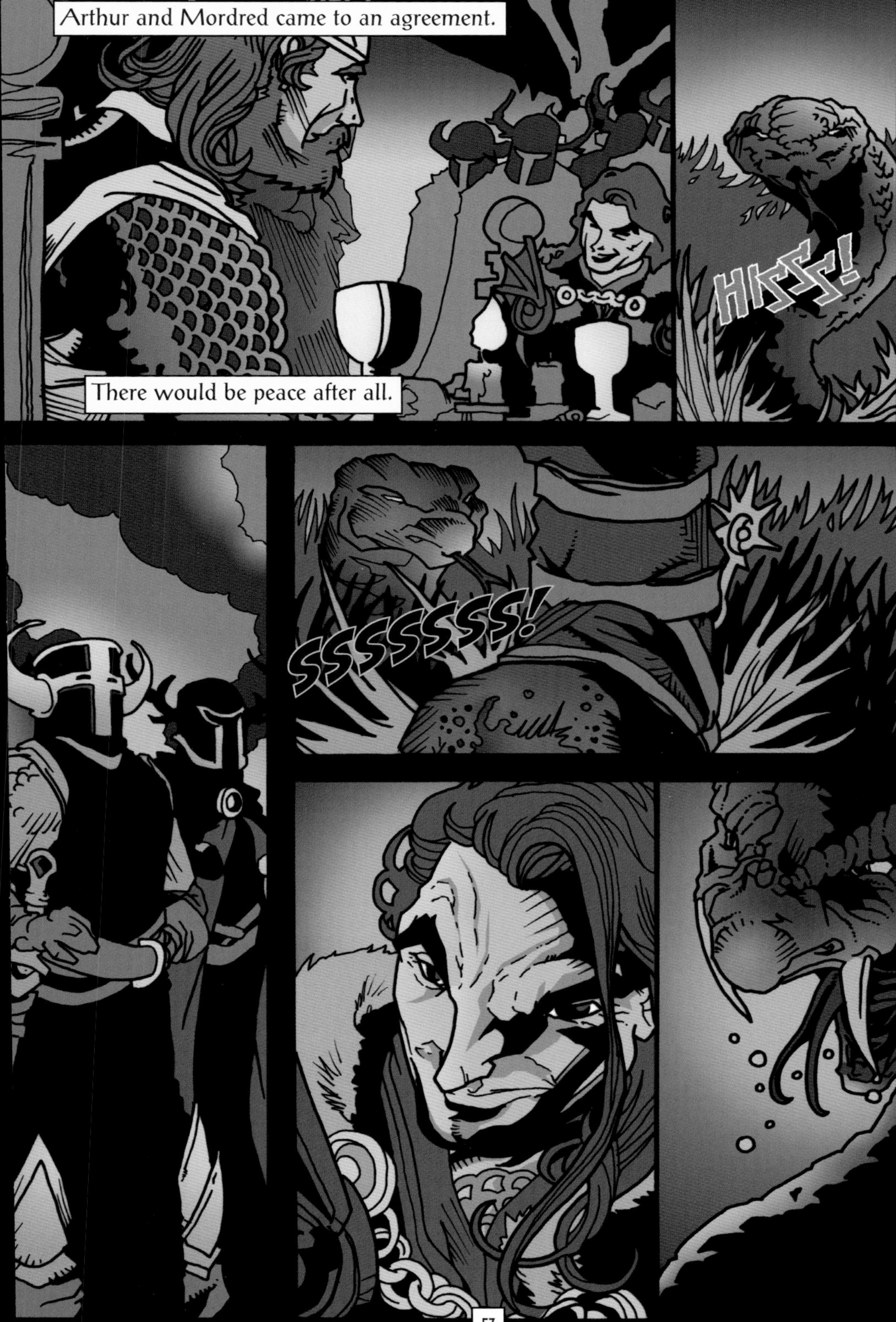
Arthur and Mordred came to an agreement.
There would be peace after all.
HISS!
SSSSSSS!

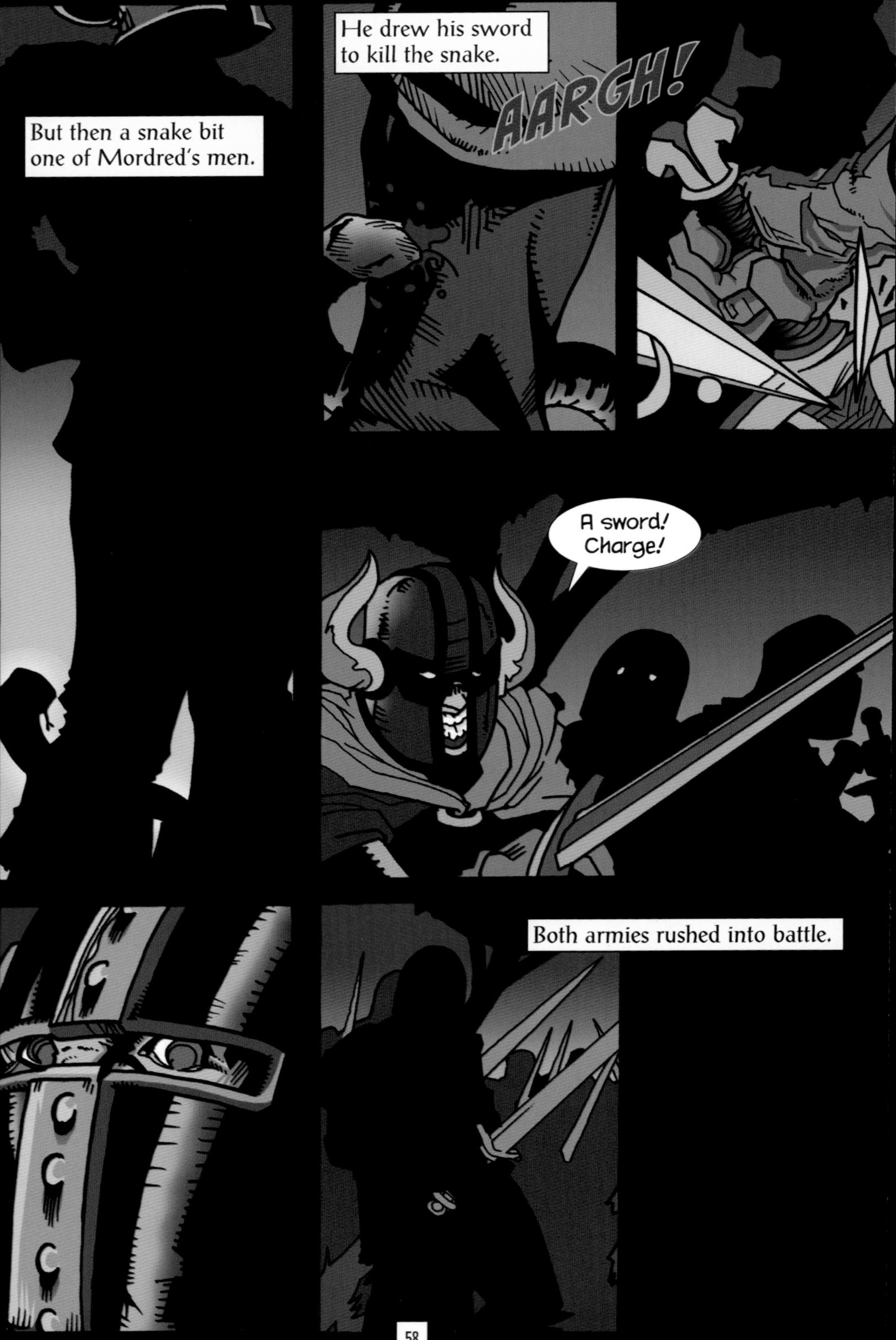
But then a snake bit one of Mordred's men.
He drew his sword to kill the snake.
AARGH!
A sword! Charge!
Both armies rushed into battle.

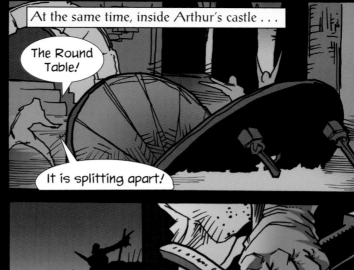

By dark, the field was covered with bodies.

My noble knights! So many lost!

At the same time, inside Arthur's castle . . .

The Round Table!

It is splitting apart!

From his vantage point, Arthur saw Mordred.

Traitor! You shall pay!

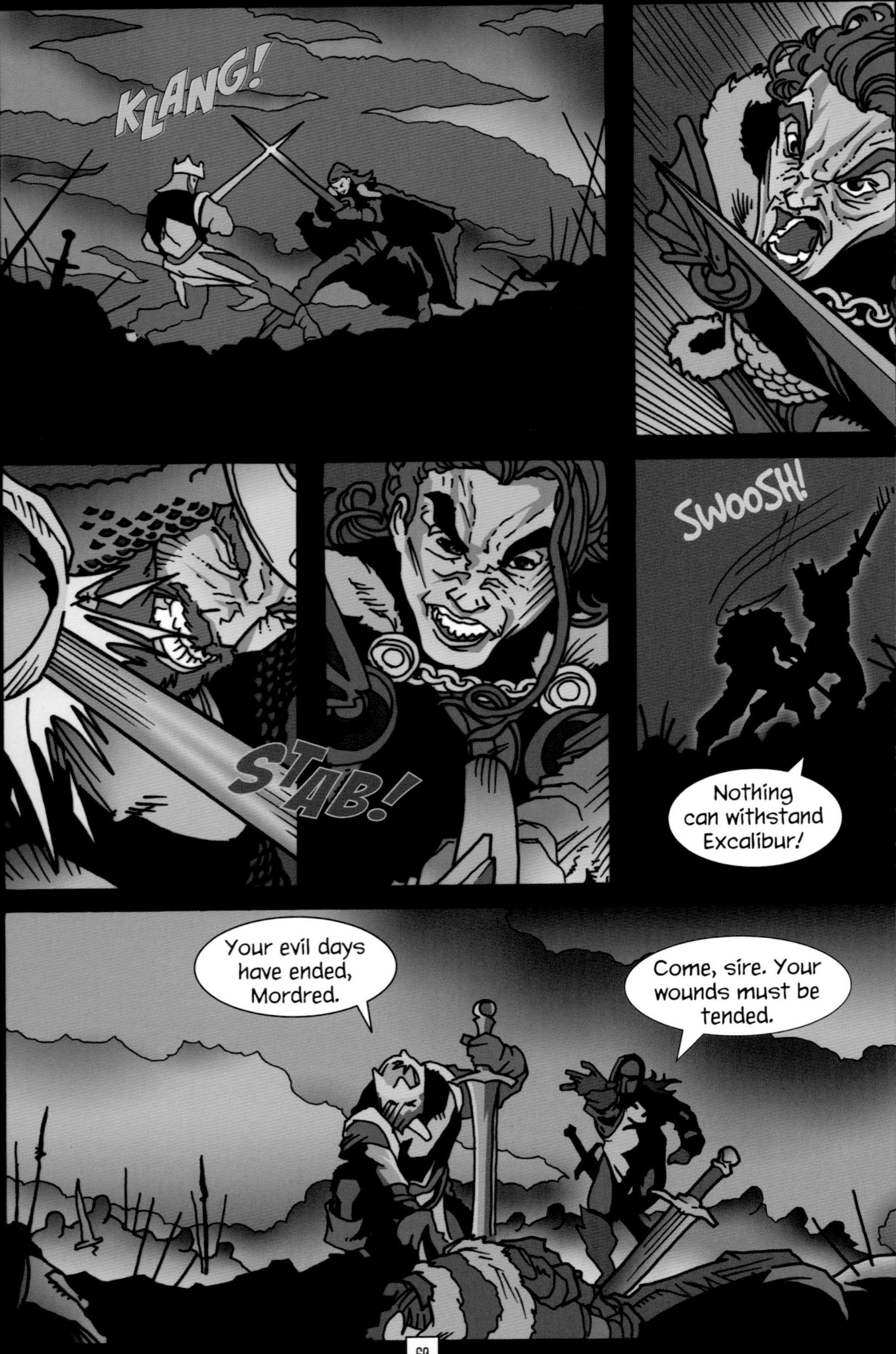
KLANG!
STAB!
SWOOSH!
Nothing can withstand Excalibur!
Your evil days have ended, Mordred.
Come, sire. Your wounds must be tended.

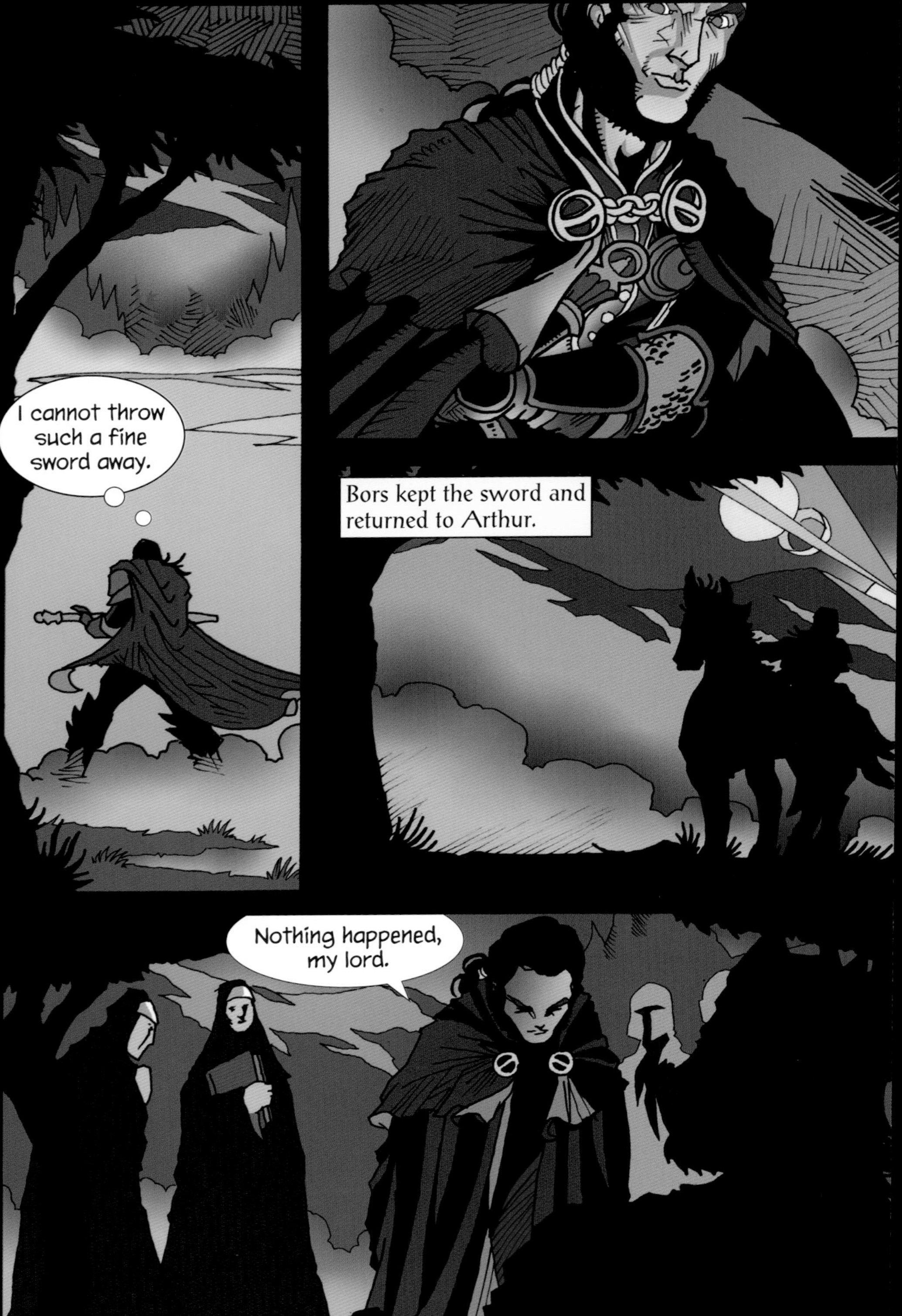
I cannot throw such a fine sword away.
Bors kept the sword and returned to Arthur.
Nothing happened, my lord.

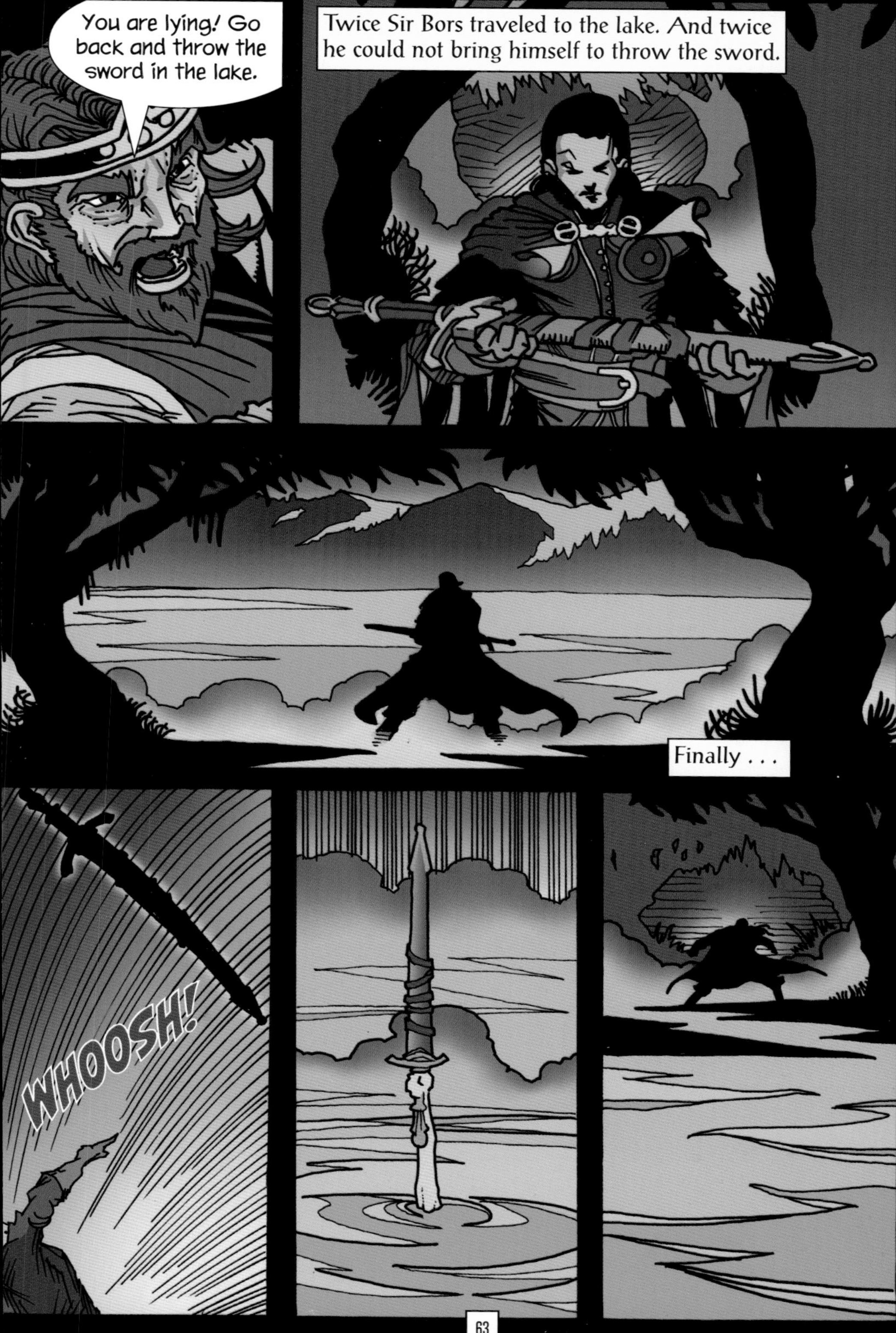
You are lying! Go back and throw the sword in the lake.
Twice Sir Bors traveled to the lake. And twice he could not bring himself to throw the sword.
Finally . . .
WHOOSH!

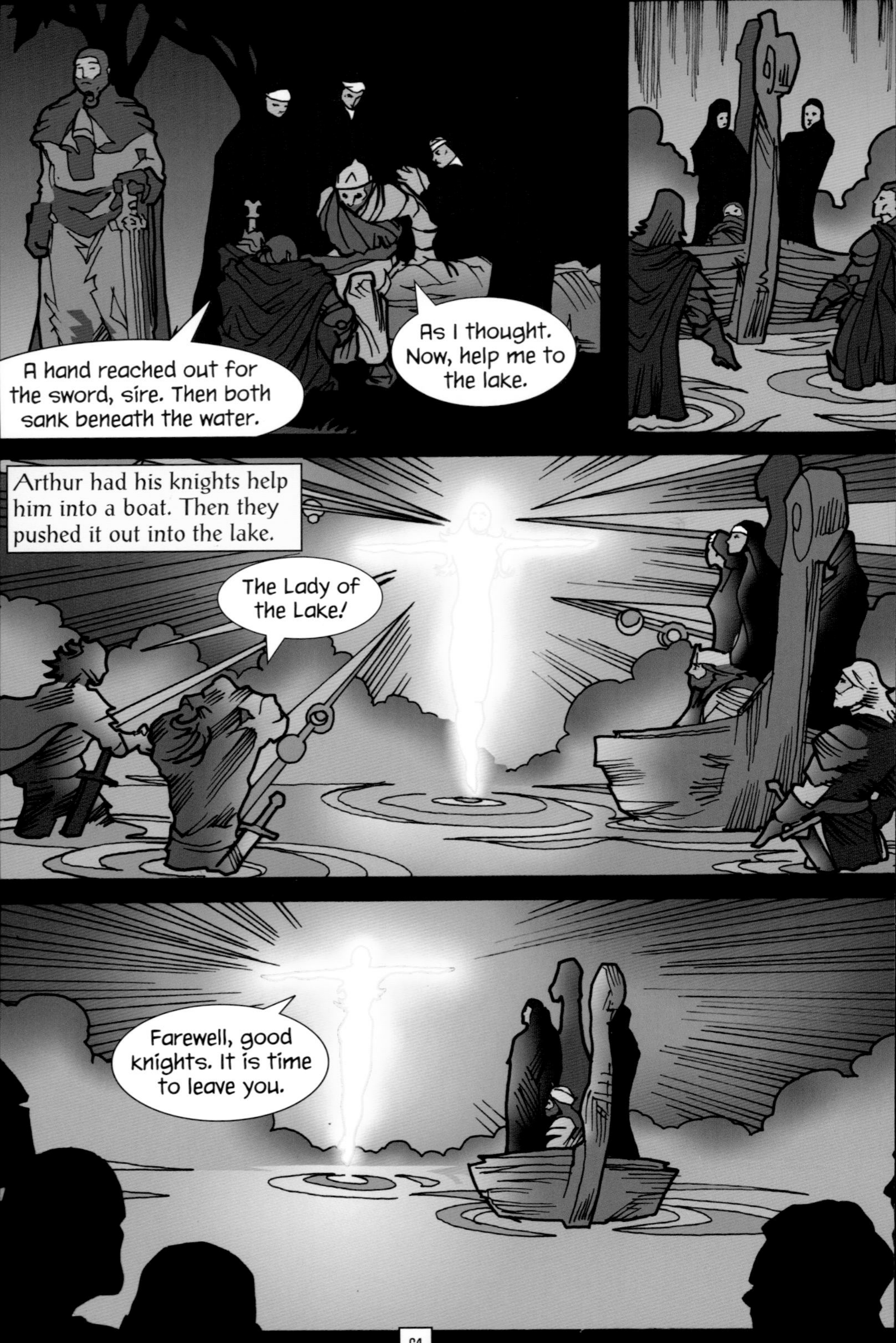
A hand reached out for the sword, sire. Then both sank beneath the water.
As I thought. Now, help me to the lake.
Arthur had his knights help him into a boat. Then they pushed it out into the lake.
The Lady of the Lake!
Farewell, good knights. It is time to leave you.

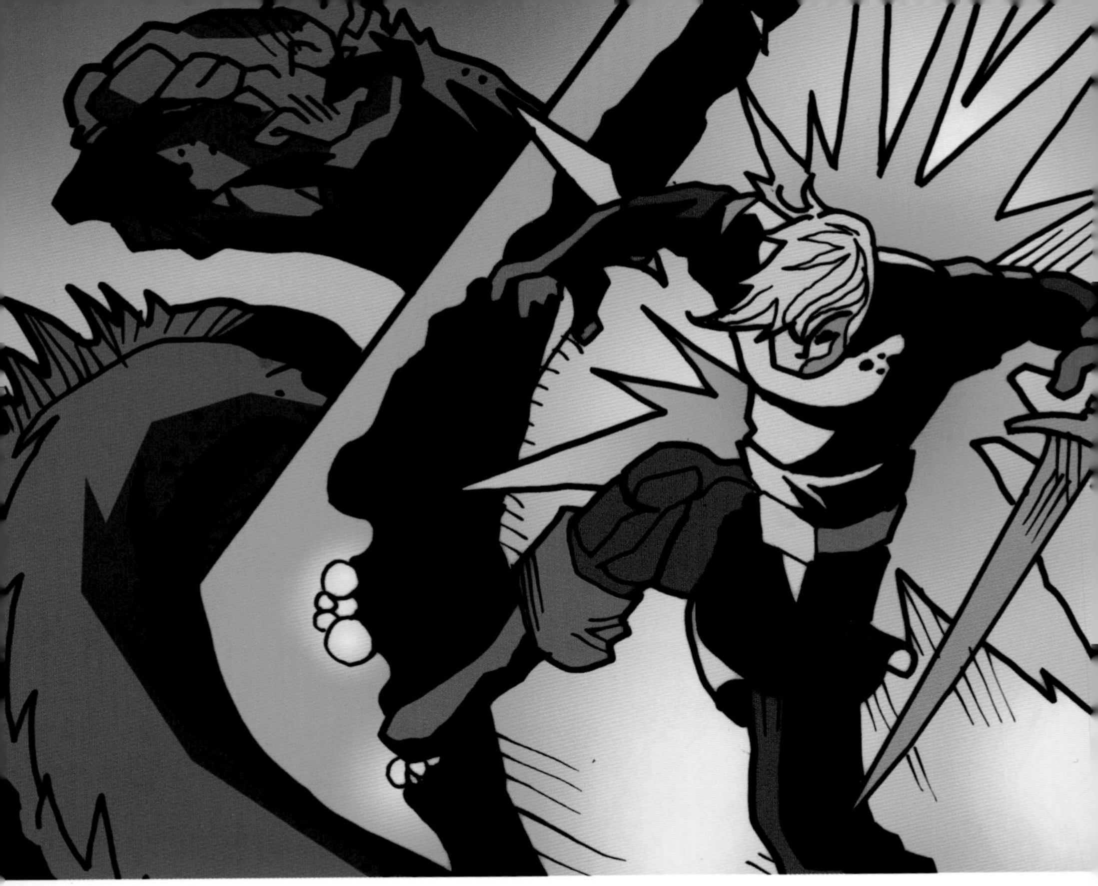

ABOUT THE RETELLING AUTHOR AND ILLUSTRATOR

M.C. Hall has written more than 80 fiction and nonfiction books for children, including science books, biographies, and fairy tales. She likes to read, walk on the beach, garden, and ski. She lives in the Boston area.

C. E. Richards grew up reading comic books, C. S. Lewis, J. R. R. Tolkien, and watching *Star Wars*. He is a graduate of Savannah College of Art and lives in Atlanta, where he is working on book and magazine illustrations, comic books, poster design, playbill illustration, and album artwork for CDs.

GLOSSARY

archbishop (arch-BISH-up)—the ruler of bishops in some Christian religions

duke (DOOK)—in Britain, a ruler ranked lower than a prince

fortress (FOR-truhss)—a group of buildings protected by walls and forts

hermit (HUR-mit)—a person who lives alone and away from others

joust (JOWST)—a battle with lances or spears fought between knights on horseback

moat (MOHT)—a deep, wide ditch filled with water that surrounds a castle or fortress and keeps people away

perilous (PARE-uhl-uhss)—dangerous

potion (PO-shuhn)—a drink with special powers

prophecy (PROF-uh-see)—a foretelling or prediction of what is going to happen

scabbard (SKAB-urd)—a case that people wear to hold a sword

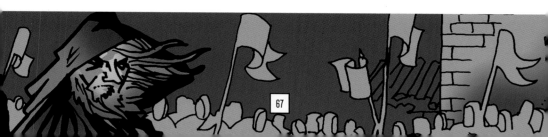

COMMON CORE ALIGNED
READING QUESTIONS

1. Write down what you know about any of the following topics that are key to this story: knights, wizards, chivalry, kings and queens, love, and battles. Have you read any other stories that use those words? Which stories? Have you ever heard any of these words before? Where and how were they used? *("By the end of the year, read and comprehend literature . . . with scaffolding as needed at the high end of the range.")*

2. Who is Lady Guinevere? Why she is important to the story? *("Describe in depth a character, setting, or event in a story.")*

3. Relationships are important to this story. What evidence in this graphic novel, especially between the characters, would lead you to think that relationships are important? *("Determine a theme of a story.")*

4. Describe Merlin. What is he like? What does he do in the story? Cite specific details in the art and text. *("Describe in depth a character . . . drawing on specific details in the text.")*

5. How does Galahad end up at the Round Table? How do Arthur and the other characters know he belongs at the famous table? *("Refer to details and examples in a text when explaining what the text says explicitly and when drawing inferences from the text.")*

COMMON CORE ALIGNED
WRITING QUESTIONS

1. Who do you think is the strongest character in the story? With evidence from the text write a one-page argument to support your choice. *("Draw evidence from literary . . . texts to support analysis.")*

2. Merlin is often mysterious and magical. If he were to visit you, what magical power would you want him to teach you? Write a one-page answer that identifies which power you would want Merlin to give you, and at least three reasons why. *("Write opinion pieces on topics or texts, supporting a point of view with reasons and information.")*

3. Choose one of your favorite characters from *King Arthur and the Knights of the Round Table* and write a new chapter to the graphic novel. Which character would you be, and what would your chapter be about? Be sure to start your new chapter where the graphic novel ends. *("Write informative/explanatory texts to examine a topic and convey ideas.")*

4. If you could be a knight of the Round Table, what kind of knight would you be? All of the knights in the story are known for a specific value or virtue (for example, Sir Galahad is known for being pure of heart). What would you be known for? Write a two-page creative story about yourself as a new knight of the Round Table. *("Write narratives to develop real or imagined experiences or events.")*

5. Pretend you are a news reporter and write a blog or online news report that explains the legendary quest for the Holy Grail. Why are they searching for the Grail? What kind of adventures do they go on? What happens during their adventures? *("Draw evidence from literary . . . texts to support analysis.")*

READ THEM ALL!

JULES VERNE'S
20,000 LEAGUES
UNDER THE SEA
A GRAPHIC NOVEL

MARK TWAIN'S
THE ADVENTURES OF
TOM SAWYER
A GRAPHIC NOVEL

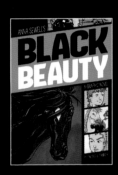

ANNA SEWELL'S
BLACK
BEAUTY
A GRAPHIC NOVEL

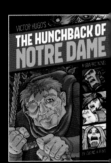

VICTOR HUGO'S
THE HUNCHBACK OF
NOTRE DAME
A GRAPHIC NOVEL

ROBIN HOOD
A GRAPHIC NOVEL

ROBERT LOUIS STEVENSON'S
TREASURE
ISLAND
A GRAPHIC NOVEL

MARY SHELLEY'S
FRANKENSTEIN
A GRAPHIC NOVEL

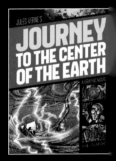

JULES VERNE'S
JOURNEY
TO THE CENTER
OF THE EARTH
A GRAPHIC NOVEL

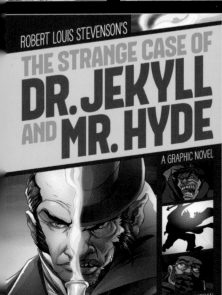

ROBERT LOUIS STEVENSON'S
THE STRANGE CASE OF
DR. JEKYLL
AND MR. HYDE
A GRAPHIC NOVEL

BY BOWEN & FERRAN

WASHINGTON IRVING'S
THE LEGEND OF
SLEEPY HOLLOW
A GRAPHIC NOVEL

BRAM STOKER'S
DRACULA

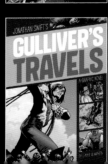

JONATHAN SWIFT'S
GULLIVER'S
TRAVELS
A GRAPHIC NOVEL

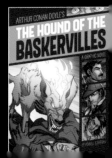

ARTHUR CONAN DOYLE'S
THE HOUND OF THE
BASKERVILLES
A GRAPHIC NOVEL

JOHANN DAVID WYSS'
THE SWISS FAMILY ROBINSON
A GRAPHIC NOVEL
PERSEUS AND MEDUSA
A GRAPHIC NOVEL
LEWIS CARROLL'S
ALICE IN WONDERLAND
A GRAPHIC NOVEL
H. G. WELLS'S
THE WAR OF THE WORLDS
A GRAPHIC NOVEL
BY MILLER & BREVARD
H.G. WELLS'S
THE TIME MACHINE
A GRAPHIC NOVEL
BY DAVIS & RUIZ
KING ARTHUR AND THE KNIGHTS OF THE ROUND TABLE
A GRAPHIC NOVEL
THE ADVENTURES OF HERCULES
A GRAPHIC NOVEL
BY POWELL & RUIZ

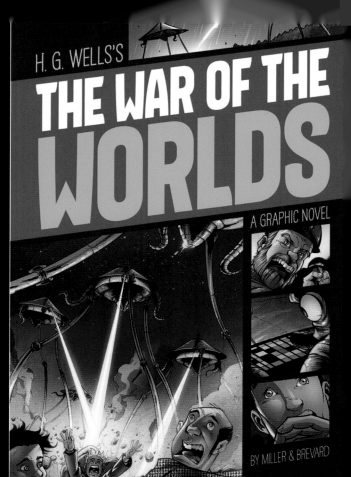

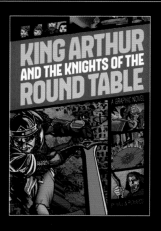

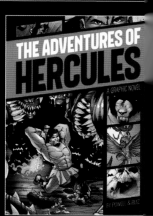